"Don't forget why we planne

Jean-Pierre's words were soft   , a gentle rumble between them while they stood so close.

"To show any nearby press that we're spending time together. That there is no bad blood between us."

"We are going to have to do better than demonstrate a lack of enmity. We need to show we're more than just friends, Tatiana. We're building a story so we can introduce our son to the world." He lowered his head closer to hers, his lips brushing her hair as he spoke into her ear. "But if you leap away every time I touch you, no one is going to buy it."

The warmth of his body next to hers awakened every nerve ending. He smelled good, like spices and fresh air. She closed her eyes for just a moment, breathing him in. She lifted her palms to his chest, touching him on instinct. And while she might tell herself that touch maintained a few inches of space between them, she knew better.

Having her hands on him was a simple pleasure too good to deny herself after the tumultuous last weeks.

"Agreed."

* * *

Secret Baby Scandal is part of the Bayou Billionaires series—secrets and scandal are a Cajun family legacy for the Reynaud brothers!

Dear Reader,

When I married a man who worked as a sports editor at a newspaper, I couldn't have possibly imagined all the ways his passion for sports would inspire and affect me. For years, I read the stories he wrote about athletes of all kinds, and I enjoyed hearing the backstory behind each one. What makes a star athlete strive? What obstacles had they faced in order to live their dreams?

As we moved from state to state, he covered high school, college and the pros. But no matter the geographic region or the level of competition, so many of the stories remained the same. Passion and hard work could trump natural born ability. There's no *I* in team. And the most successful stars had all made huge sacrifices to get where they were.

Long after my husband moved on to other interests, the stories remained with me. Of course, in my world, there's always a woman involved! I hope you enjoy them as much as I have. I gifted this hero, Jean-Pierre Reynaud, with a wealth of athletic abilities. But no man can live on sports alone, so Tatiana Doucet arrives in his life in time to shake things up a bit.

Happy reading,

Joanne Rock

JOANNE ROCK

SECRET BABY SCANDAL

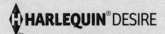

HARLEQUIN®DESIRE

Recycling programs
for this product may
not exist in your area

ISBN-13: 978-0-373-73458-0

Secret Baby Scandal

Copyright © 2016 by Joanne Rock

Printed in U.S.A.

www.Harlequin.com

Three-time RITA® Award nominee **Joanne Rock** has penned over sixty stories for Harlequin. An optimist by nature and perpetual seeker of silver linings, Joanne finds romance fits her life outlook perfectly—love is worth fighting for. A former Golden Heart® Award recipient, she has won numerous awards for her stories. Learn more about Joanne's imaginative Muse by visiting her website joannerock.com or follow @joannerock6 on Twitter.

Books by Joanne Rock

HARLEQUIN DESIRE

Bayou Billionaires

His Secretary's Surprise Fiancé
Secret Baby Scandal

HARLEQUIN BLAZE

Double Play
Under Wraps
Highly Charged!
Making a Splash
Riding the Storm
One Man Rush
Her Man Advantage
Full Surrender
My Double Life
A Soldier's Christmas
"Presents Under the Tree"
My Secret Fantasies

Visit her Author Profile page at Harlequin.com, or joannerock.com, for more titles.

To the Desire authors and editors who made me feel so welcome in this series long before my first book hit the shelves. Thank you!

One

"Good game, Reynaud." The beat writer who covered the New York Gladiators waited with a microphone in hand as starting quarterback, Jean-Pierre Reynaud, stepped into the interview room at the Coliseum Sports Complex.

Jean-Pierre was prepared for the reporter's questions as he settled into a canvas director's chair in the small, glassed-in booth after his third straight win at home. Just outside the interview room, thousands of fans lingered in the Coliseum's Coaches Club, staying after the game to see the players take turns answering questions for the media. Here, fans could relax and have a drink at the bar while the traffic thinned out after the Sunday night matchup versus Philadelphia.

After clipping the small microphone onto his jacket lapel with his right hand, which not too long ago had thrown the game-winning pass, Jean-Pierre gave the crowd a quick wave. The high ticket prices for the exclusive Coaches Club didn't prevent the fans here from bringing glittery signs or asking for autographs, but team security made sure these kinds of events went smoothly. Jean-Pierre would give an interview and roll out of here in less than thirty minutes, which would leave enough time to catch a private plane to New Orleans tonight. He needed to take care of some Reynaud family business, for one thing.

And for another? He planned to discreetly scout his brother's team, the New Orleans Hurricanes, before the much touted brother-against-brother football showdown in week twelve of the regular season. Of the four Reynaud siblings, Jean-Pierre's eldest brother, Gervais, owned the Hurricanes. The next oldest, Dempsey, coached the Hurricanes. And Henri Reynaud, known league-wide as the Bayou Bomber, ran the Hurricanes' offense from the quarterback position, slinging record-setting pass yardage with an arm destined for hall-of-fame greatness.

Living up to that legacy? No big deal. Right?

Damn.

As the youngest member of Louisiana's wealthiest family and co-owner of the Reynaud Shipping empire, Jean-Pierre had inherited his love of the game from his father and his grandfather, the same as his brothers. But he was the player the New Orleans papers liked to call "the Louisiana Turncoat" for daring to forge a career outside his home state—and outside of his family's sphere of influence. But since no NFL club had ever successfully split the starting QB job between two players, and Jean-Pierre wasn't the kind of man to play in a brother's shadow, he didn't care what the Big Easy sports pundits had to say about that. When the Gladiators made him an offer, he'd taken it gladly…once he'd recovered from the shock, of course. Gladiators head coach Jack Doucet had been an enemy of the Reynauds after a football-related falling-out between their families. Jack had been the second in command back on a Texas team that Jean-Pierre's grandfather had owned, and not only had the split been acrimonious, but it had also severed Jean-Pierre's brief prep-school romance with Jack's daughter when they moved across the country.

So yeah, it had been a surprise when Jack's team had offered Jean-Pierre a contract with the Gladiators.

New York was a big enough stage to prove himself worthy of the family's football legacy, but there was no room for failure. No NFL team sat in a brighter spotlight—the Gladiators doled out the highest number of press passes to media members. And if Jean-Pierre didn't hold their interest? He lost ink—and fans—to the second NFL club in New York, the one he got stuck sharing a stadium with on the weekends. He'd learned to play the press as well as he played his position on the field, was unwilling to lose the traction he'd gained since arriving in the Big Apple.

"Are you ready?" a New York sports radio personality asked him as the number of interviewers around him multiplied.

Jean-Pierre nodded, shoving his still-damp hair off his forehead before straightening his tie. The fast showers after a game barely took the steam off him. His muscles remained hot long afterward, especially since he did the interviews in suit and tie. His silk jacket weighed on his shoulders like a stack of wool blankets after two hours on the field dodging hits from the fastest D-line in the game.

Around him, the room quieted. The doors had been secured. Waiting for the first question to be fired his way, he peered past the reporters to the fans in the Coaches Club. All around the space, huge televisions that normally broadcast the game were now filled with the feed from the interview room. Jean-Pierre's gaze roamed over to where the team owner sat, holding court at one end of the bar with a handful of minor celebrities and a few of the first-year players.

And just when he needed his focus most, that's when he glimpsed *her*.

The head coach's daughter, Tatiana Doucet.

Infuriating. Sexy. And completely off-limits.

Their impulsive one-night stand last year had wrecked any chance they might have had at recovering their friendship. But dammit all, just looking at her still set his body on fire in a way that tripled any heat lingering from his time on the field.

He tugged at his tie and took in the sight of her, unable to tear his eyes away.

Tall and lean, she wore one of those dresses that showed off mile-long legs. Even though the rest of the dress was modest—splashes of colors highlighted with sequins, neckline up to her throat, sleeves that hit her wrist—the acres of bare skin from the middle of her thigh that trailed south were enough to stop traffic. She wore a silk scarf around her hair like a headband, no doubt to hold back the riot of dark brown curls that brushed her shoulders. Curls he remembered plunging his hands into during the best sex of his life. She stood at the back of the room, hovering close to an exit as if she wanted to be ready to run at first sight of him.

He understood that feeling well.

The punch to his chest from just *seeing* her was so strong he missed the first question in the interview, the words a warble of background noise in his head. How long had it been since she'd shown up at any Gladiators event?

Not since last season. Jean-Pierre hadn't laid eyes on her since that ill-advised night they'd spent tearing off each other's clothes.

Ignoring the aggravating rush of air though his lungs at spotting the woman he'd once cared about—a woman who'd since traded her soul for the sake of her job as a trial attorney—Jean-Pierre focused on the man holding the microphone.

"Run that question by me again?" He hitched the heel of his shoe on the metal bar of the director's chair and tried to get comfortable and relax into the interview the way he always did, even though his pulse hammered hard and his temperature spiked.

A low rumble of laughter from the journalists told Jean-Pierre he'd missed something. The throng crowded him, the handheld mics pushing closer while the boom mic overhead lowered a fraction. The sudden tension in the air was thick and palpable.

"No doubt it's a question you can't prepare for." The reporter from Gladiators TV, a popular app for mobile users, grinned at him. "But I have to ask what you think of Tatiana Doucet's remark to me just a minute ago, that she wouldn't bet against the Bayou Bomber playing in his home state when you match up against your brother's team in week twelve?"

The words sunk in. Hard. They damn near knocked him back in his chair.

Tatiana had said that? Implying she *would* bet against the Gladiators, the team her father coached? Or, more precisely, she would bet against Jean-Pierre.

Her father was going to have a conniption over that remark. Not just because of the suggestion that anyone in his family would bet on a game in any way, which was strictly forbidden. Jack Doucet would also spit nails over the fact that his own daughter was generating media hype in favor of an opponent.

Jean-Pierre didn't spare a glance to see the head coach's

reaction in real time out in the Coaches Club, however. He'd been giving interviews too long to get caught flat-footed twice in a row. He wasn't about to let the media play him over a thoughtless remark Tatiana must have uttered with no regard to who might overhear. Hell no. Instead, he spouted the first scrap of damage control his brain had to offer.

"My guess is that Miss Doucet would like to fire up the Gladiators and help us play our best, even if that means putting a little good-natured ribbing into the mix." He flashed his most careless grin in a performance worthy of an Academy Award given the way she'd just kicked his teeth in.

Ten reporters asked questions at the same time, the cacophony making it hard to hear what anyone was saying. They ended up deferring to the *New York Post* reporter, a cantankerous older guy who scared off any journalist who hadn't been around since the typewriter era.

"C'mon, Reynaud," he growled, a sour expression on his face while he took notes in longhand. "Her words don't sound playful to me. When even the coach's daughter doesn't believe in you—"

"Hey. You can stop right there." Jean-Pierre cut the guy off, unwilling to let him stir the pot with that line of questioning. "Tatiana and I went to school together and I know her well. I guarantee she was joking." He sensed the unrest in the room despite his reassurances. This remark was the kind of thing that overshadowed games. Teams. Whole freaking seasons. And he was not going to allow one superficial remark to steal the spotlight from the Gladiators' hard work.

So he lied through his teeth.

"In fact," he continued, never allowing that fake smile to falter, "Tatiana will be going with me to New Orleans as a special guest of the Reynaud family during the bye week. She can't wait to visit Bayou country again."

He glanced outside the glass to where she'd been standing earlier, but she had disappeared. No doubt she hadn't wanted to field follow-up questions. Or answer to her father.

Or see him? Yes, that bothered him more than it should. But he couldn't deny he missed her.

When they were teenagers, Tatiana had spent two years at a prep school half an hour away from the Reynaud family compound. Consequently, she'd visited his house on the shore of Lake Pontchartrain plenty of times when they were younger.

The beat of silence following Jean-Pierre's announcement might have been laughable if he hadn't needed the time to brace himself for round two of the questions that didn't have a damn thing to do with the game he'd just played. But he'd set them all back on their heels for a second.

"A guest of the *family* or of yours?"

One reporter barely finished speaking before the next question.

"Does it bother you that she prosecuted your old teammate in a sexual harassment suit last winter?"

"Is she invited to your brother's wedding?"

Reporters were talking over each other again, firing off questions left and right, but this time Jean-Pierre could pick out a few of them. He had no intention of discussing the weeks he and Tatiana had sat on opposite sides of a tense courtroom while she used all her talents as an attorney to win a civil suit against one of his old friends. As for the wedding, Gervais planned to marry a foreign princess in New Orleans during the team's bye week—the week neither the Gladiators nor the Hurricanes played.

But since Gervais and his fiancée had done all they could to keep the details private, that question would go unanswered, too. Still, Jean-Pierre didn't mind letting the press assume Tatiana was his guest for that event.

For that matter, he would have to make sure she was his real date for his brother's nuptials. No way would the media interest in them die without serious effort from both of them. Their fiery past would have to take a backseat because he couldn't let her derail his career.

She knew the politics of this world well enough to understand a comment like hers simply couldn't stand. She would have to help put out the fire she'd started. God only knew why she'd done it since she was normally as cautious in her personal life as she was in the courtroom.

"Any questions you would like to ask me about the game?" Jean-Pierre asked, figuring he'd given them enough to refute Tatiana's earlier remark.

His gaze slid to the Coaches Club and he noticed that both Jack and his daughter had disappeared. No doubt Tatiana's father was giving her hell somewhere privately. But then, her old man had always put football before family. He was an okay guy to play for once they'd gotten past the old Reynaud-Doucet rift, but that sure didn't make him a good father.

Jean-Pierre fielded a few more interview questions, quickly outlining his decision-making for a couple of passes that he'd thrown and discussing a controversial pass-interference call. Then he was on his feet and unclipping the mic for the next player, the Gladiators' Pro-Bowl star safety, Tevon Alvarez.

"That was some serious grace under pressure, dude," Tevon muttered in Jean-Pierre's ear as he clapped him on the shoulder. "You're my idol with the hacks."

"I'm used to facing the meanest defensive ends in the

NFL every week," he told him. "The hacks aren't nearly as scary."

Jean-Pierre stepped into the private tunnel leading toward the players' lounge, but midway through, he doubled back toward the Coaches Club. He'd approach it from the private entrance, close to where the Gladiators administration kept a couple of offices.

Because there wasn't a chance in hell he was leaving this stadium without talking to Tatiana first. She might have successfully ducked him since last winter, but with her remark to the media tonight, she'd put herself right back in his world. Now he planned to keep her there for however long it took for this new scandal to die down.

In her professional life, Tatiana Doucet had often been praised for her cool head and ability to organize her thoughts into a reasoned, intelligent argument. So it seemed unfair that on the day when she needed to make the most important and *private* announcement of her life, she'd wound up nervously babbling to a reporter, of all people. In public.

Standing outside the New York Gladiators postgame press event, Tatiana folded a cocktail napkin into her palm and mopped it across her forehead. What had she been thinking to spout such an offhand comment to a stranger across from her at the ice-cream-sundae bar? She hadn't seen the reporter's press pass—he must have taken it off. Although clearly he hadn't turned off his recorder. Looking back, it seemed obvious the guy had been baiting her to make a comment about the upcoming Hurricanes game.

And she'd played right into his hands because she'd been nervous about seeing Jean-Pierre. She'd accidentally given a sound bite that would be all the New York sports media talked about for weeks. Her father would strangle her when he found her. But so far, she'd eluded him. The subterranean hallways of the Coliseum were narrow and echoed, making it easy to stay one step ahead of a coach charging around like an angry bull.

But while she'd put off a confrontation with her dad, she couldn't afford to delay the conversation she needed to have with another man who would have every reason to be angry with her.

Gladiators starting quarterback, Jean-Pierre Reynaud.

She hadn't stayed in the Coaches Club long enough to hear how Jean-Pierre responded to the reporter who'd blindsided him with her remark. She'd turned on her heels and booked out of there. But somehow, she needed to find Jean-Pierre before she left tonight. Her private announcement was for his ears only.

She'd justified staying away from him after their one night together last winter, since their parting had been as passionate as the sex, although not nearly as fulfilling. They had a tumultuous history, considering their prep-school romance that had failed thanks to their families' well-documented enmity. Then, after meeting up years later, they'd been on opposite sides of a prominent sexual harassment case she'd prosecuted a year ago against Jean-Pierre's former teammate. Jean-Pierre had been in the courtroom almost every day after practice until she'd won a verdict against the retired football player. She'd been flush with the professional victory until a coldly furious Jean-Pierre confronted her to inform her she'd ruined an innocent man's reputation.

Even now, she didn't understand how their argument had turned into the most passionate encounter she'd ever experienced, but she sure understood his icy parting words the next morning.

That mistake will never be repeated.

She'd been cooking him breakfast at the time and hoping for…what? That they might have a shot at understanding each other even though their romantic history had proved them incompatible before they were twenty years old? Stubborn pride and embarrassment at her foolishness had kept her mouth shut for months. But tonight, she needed to set aside her old hurts and face him once and for all.

The sooner she got this over with, the better, since she needed to head home. Standing on the narrow threshold of a closed door in a deserted corridor of offices, Tatiana debated where to find her quarry. Surely he wouldn't have lingered around the Coaches Club. Maybe she could ask the security guard outside the players' lounge where Jean-Pierre was. Or would she be better off staking out his car in the parking garage? That way she could be sure she wouldn't miss him.

Darting back the way she came, she turned a corner and nearly plowed right into none other than Jean-Pierre himself.

"Oh!" With a yelp of surprise, she gripped his forearm to stay upright.

"Shh," Jean-Pierre warned her, tucking her under his arm and pressing a finger to her lips. "There's a camera crew just down that hallway." He nodded to the ramp just ahead on his right.

Tatiana tensed at his touch. His scent. His maleness. She'd spent so long avoiding him, but in spite of all logic, he affected her. At six-three, and at this close range, he had to peer down at her, his brown eyes flecked with hints of gold and green. She'd fallen for him hard back in prep school, a young love that had only felt more poignant after they'd been torn apart by their families' sudden rift. They'd both moved on, of course, two thousand miles of separation proving as effective a deterrent as the well-publicized feud. But when he'd joined the Gladiators and she'd seen him at the occasional party, she'd been as drawn to him as ever. It had been an attraction that hadn't been reciprocated, judging by his cold words about her court case last winter. She still didn't understand how that terse confrontation in the courtroom had turned so heated.

Now, heart hammering, she simply nodded, knowing they needed to avoid the press. Heaven forbid the media were to overhear what she had to tell Jean-Pierre.

He frowned down at her, not moving.

"What?" she whispered, shaky and off balance as she peered up into his shadowed face.

"We could let them find us," he suggested, his gaze roving over her as he seemed to weigh the idea. "They could photograph us kissing."

The mention of kissing should not have sent a bolt of lightning through her. Especially when Jean-Pierre seemed to be mulling over the idea with the same attention he might give a playbook. Dispassionate. Assessing.

"Are you insane?" Her whisper notched up an octave as she grabbed his sleeve and tugged him in the other direction.

Not that he moved.

"It would end the speculation that we're enemies," he said. They stood facing each other in silence for a moment until she could hear the echo of footsteps in the northern corridor.

"We *are* enemies," she reminded him, tugging his arm with more urgency. "Just because you and my father patched things up enough for you to play in New York doesn't mean the Reynauds and Doucets suddenly became friends. When your grandfather fired my father from his old director-of-personnel position with the Mustangs, it might as well have been an act of war."

Her father had moved the whole family across the country, pulling her out of school and demanding an end to her relationship with Jean-Pierre. And if her father hadn't been adamant enough, her mother had been downright immovable on the subject. Seventeen at the time, Tatiana had fallen in line and put Jean-Pierre in her past…right up until that day he'd approached her after court and her old feelings had spun out of control for one passionate night.

"You think I don't remember?" He fell into step beside her now, guiding her deeper into the private areas of the stadium. "But I'd call us casualties of that battle, not enemies. And either way, I would have preferred to lock down any mentions of bad blood to the media."

He nodded to one of the guards outside the locker rooms as they passed a secured area.

"I realize that." Her heart hummed along at high speed even as she warned herself to be coolheaded. To ignore the feel of his hand on her waist when he ushered her through the heavy steel door that led to the parking garage. "I'm out of practice dealing with the media or I never would have been so flippant with a stranger. Obviously, I know better. I apologize."

His terse nod gave away nothing.

"I'm parked over here." He hit the fob on his key chain and the lights on a nearby gray Aston Martin coupe flashed twice. "I can give you a ride home and we'll…talk."

She wondered at that meaningful pause. Was he still stewing about her comment to the reporter? Regardless, she needed to do some talking of her own.

"Thank you." The clamminess that she'd felt on her skin earlier returned. Her time to tell him was running out. "I took a car service to the game so I appreciate the ride."

She'd timed her arrival so that she wouldn't set foot in the stadium until a few minutes before the game ended, hoping to avoid her father and spend as little time away from home as possible.

The tail end of the silk scarf she'd tied around her head caught on one of the sequins of her dress and she struggled to untangle it as she walked to his car. She was hot, tired and out of sorts, so it was no surprise that she popped a whole row of sequins off. They bounced around the floor of the parking garage while Jean-Pierre held open the door of his sports car.

It wasn't fair that he looked impeccable in a custom Hugo Boss suit while her life frayed at the seams. With an impatient swipe, she slid the scarf off her hair and lowered herself into the leather seat.

When he came around to the driver's side, he wasted no time putting the car into Reverse and heading out the exit. Game traffic had thinned out by now, putting them on the highway in no time. At this rate, in ten more minutes they'd be at her front door. Her stomach tightened at how fast her time was running out to make her cool, calm announcement. If she could even remember that speech she'd practiced in her mind a thousand times. She toyed with the fringe on the edges of her silk scarf, watching the play of pink, green and blue threads over her fingers.

"You didn't hear my answers in that interview, did you?" Jean-Pierre said suddenly, diverting her thoughts.

"No, I'm afraid not." She seized on the reprieve with both hands. "I ditched the Coaches Club the second I recognized that reporter's face on the big screen over the bar. I knew he was about to corner you with what I'd just told him, so I left before my father could blow a gasket and blast me in front of five thousand fans."

She studied Jean-Pierre's expression in the dashboard

lights, his chiseled profile deep in five-o'clock shadow and a fresh scrape visible on his right cheekbone. He'd been lucky today. She'd spent enough time in her father's world to see the toll that football could take on the strongest men.

"I told the media you were joking." He glanced at her as they neared signs for the Lincoln Tunnel.

"Of course I was. I thought I was talking to a Gladiators fan and I was just messing around." She knew from experience she didn't need to stroke this man's ego, but she also didn't like the idea that he might think she'd been in earnest. "Obviously you and Henri are supremely well-matched. If you played ten games, I'd give you each five."

"Very generous of you." He downshifted as traffic slowed in a sea of brake lights. "And probably accurate given our stats in backyard games. But back to the interview. I not only told the reporter you were joking, I also assured him you were going to be my guest for the bye week and that you couldn't wait to return to Louisiana for a visit."

He said it so tonelessly that she hoped she'd misheard. Surely he wouldn't have done that. He didn't even *like* her anymore. He'd made sure she knew as much when he'd walked out of her home the last time.

"No. You. Didn't." The words were a soft scrape of air, her voice vanishing as they entered the tunnel, the regular intervals of fluorescent light flashing through the car and making her dizzy.

"Oh, yes, I most certainly did. What would you have suggested I say, Tatiana?" His grip on the wheel tightened for a moment before he loosened his hold again. He removed one hand from the wheel altogether and flexed his knuckles, as if forcing himself to relax. Or maybe he was nursing an injury.

And, oh, God, how could he have just told the whole world they were going to be spending a week together?

"I just—" She swallowed hard. Tried to channel her inner lawyer and come up with a quietly reasoned argument. But all the arguments that came to mind were conversational dynamite. "That can't happen," she said lamely.

"And yet, we'll have to make a good show of it since your comment could cause the kind of media uproar that steals focus away from a team. I can't afford that distraction right now." He lifted a hand to his tie and loosened the knot, looking for all the world like a dissolute playboy with his unshaven jaw in his sexy car.

But looks were deceiving, and nothing about this man was dissolute or inclined to play. It didn't matter that his weekly contests were labeled "games," Jean-Pierre Reynaud was one of the most serious and hardworking men she'd ever met. He was relentless in achieving what he wanted, in fact. So she understood immediately that he wouldn't back down on the good show for the media now that he'd promised it.

"You don't understand—" she began, only to be cut short.

"It might be you who doesn't understand." He steered off the exit toward 42nd Street and she wished she could turn back the clock on this evening to make the outcome different. To give her more time. She took in his tight jaw, his tense shoulders. "I didn't have time to consult you for a plan. You put me on the spot in front of my team, the league, the media and the fans."

"You're right. That part, I do understand." Her breasts ached beneath her dress, the need to return home a sudden, biological need. Thankfully, all the lights on 10th Avenue went green and they surged through one after the other as they headed north.

"Excellent. You are already invited to my brother's wedding." He resumed laying out the calm, controlled plan that she knew would never happen. "We can attend the ceremony together and then you will stay in New Orleans until the Gladiators game against the Hurricanes the week after. I'll have to commute back and forth for practices, but I'll be around enough to ensure we're photographed together. We can put a quick end to the old rumors about our families. And about us."

Only a Reynaud would seriously contemplate "commuting" between New York and New Orleans. She would have laughed if she hadn't been so upset, rapidly bordering on panicked. But she'd certainly learned how to deal with unexpected consequences. Now, Jean-Pierre would have to learn, too.

"Fine," she agreed rather than waste her breath arguing, already knowing whatever plans he made now were about to be blown up anyhow. "You may not want me in New Orleans with you once you hear what I have to say." She gritted her teeth as they hit Central Park West and neared her building. The ache in her chest shifted painfully. "Would you come in with me so we can continue this discussion inside?"

"Of course. We have a lot of plans to make." He pulled in alongside the valet and handed over his keys.

On the elevator, she realized she had effectively put off her important announcement so long that very soon no words would be necessary and she would lose her window to tell Jean-Pierre herself. She wasn't proud of that. But she was tired, aching and uncomfortable. And didn't he bear half the blame for this impossible situation?

Yet, as soon as the elevator stopped on her floor and the doors slid open, she knew she couldn't let him find out this way.

"We do have a lot of plans to make." She spun to face him, the words spilling out fast. "But not the kind you think."

"I don't understand." His jaw flexed, his gaze narrowing.

She drew in a deep breath.

"Remember that night last winter?" She didn't wait for his reply, as she heard a long, high-pitched wail from inside her apartment. "I should have told you sooner, but you walked out the next day and said it was a mistake. Talking was all but impossible after a parting like that and then, well—" She shook her head, impatient with herself and the excuses that didn't matter now, with her baby crying on the other side of her front door. "Come and meet your son, Jean-Pierre."

Two

Son?

Jean-Pierre had taken hits from the toughest, strongest, meanest players in the NFL. Afterward, as he lay in the grass with his ears ringing and his vision blurred, he would struggle to snap out of the slow-motion fog that felt kind of like being underwater.

That was exactly how he felt walking into Tatiana's apartment, her words slowly permeating his consciousness along with the cry of an infant. Dazed, confused and trying to stand up straight despite the floor shifting under his feet, Jean-Pierre stood in her foyer and waited for her to return from wherever she'd disappeared.

"Mr. Reynaud?" An older woman in a simple gray dress stepped into the living area to his right. "Miss Doucet asked if you wouldn't mind joining her in the family room. It's just past the staircase on the left." She pointed the way and then went about her business, picking up a few things in the living room.

A bright blue blanket. A baby bottle.

Seeing that bottle was like the second hit when you were already down.

At the same time, it was enough to make the mental fog evaporate and get his feet moving.

Fast.

He needed answers now. Hell, he needed answers months ago. Tatiana had done a whole lot more than throw his career into a tailspin tonight with her unguarded remark to a member of the press. She'd been hiding the biggest possible secret that was going to bind their lives together forever.

"Tatiana?" Her name was a sharp bark on his lips as he entered the spacious suite overlooking Central Park.

Framed playbills lined the walls along with photos of Tatiana and her family. Tatiana with her father at her graduation from Columbia. The Doucets outside of a downtown skyscraper with the brass name plaque of her prestigious law firm. Every picture was a reminder of the life he might have had with her if her family hadn't turned her against him.

A blaze crackled in a fireplace on the far side of the living area. And beside it, in that warm glow of flickering light, he spotted her on the dark leather love seat, cradling a tiny bundle of blankets to her breast. Tatiana's dark brown curls shielded her body as much as the blanket, the firelight making the skin of one shoulder glow where she'd unfastened her dress to feed the baby.

Her baby.

His…son.

Something shifted inside Jean-Pierre, his whole world tipping on its axis as everything changed irreversibly.

"I am sorry," she said softly, her hand shifting to cover a tiny foot kicking free of the cotton bundle. "I left New

York in my sixth month so that no one would find out. I wanted you to be the first to know."

He had moved deeper into the room, drawn to the sight of woman and child, trying like hell to focus on them and what they meant for him. To him. But his brain was scrambling to catch up on nearly a year's worth of living in mere moments.

"What about your family?" Had he been playing games for Jack Doucet's team while the guy kept this news hidden from him? If so, it was going to blow the Doucet-Reynaud feud wide-open again, because Jean-Pierre could not deal with that kind of duplicity. Lowering himself to the chair across from her, he sat with his back to the view of Central Park at night, his eyes on the only thing that mattered. He needed Tatiana to keep talking. To explain why he had no knowledge of this development in their lives.

"They only know I took an extended vacation. I couldn't tell them before I told you."

The tone she used suggested that was the only sensible approach, when in fact, none of this made sense to him. Who kept this kind of news from their family? Jean-Pierre might not be as close to his brothers as he once was, but damn straight they wouldn't keep something like this from each other. He'd told her how much a secret like this had hurt his own family—had hurt his half brother. "I think I'm going to need you to spell this out for me more thoroughly."

"I had so many things to organize," she continued. "I needed a good midwife. And at first I requested a leave from my job. But then I realized I needed to change my role with the law practice so that I'd be doing legal research and writing briefs instead of taking cases to trial." Her eyes were bright and worried as they flashed up to his.

At least she seemed to understand how thin her reasons sounded. But then, she'd always placed a higher priority on appearances than him. The framed photos on the walls around her sure never showed a single misstep in her perfect life. He wouldn't be surprised if the pregnancy had thrown her into a panic trying to find a way to tell her parents.

"Where did you go when you left New York?" He knew he needed to process this fast. To move past the shock of what she was telling him and start being a support to her and this new reality. But the truth of the situation was like waves at high tide, thrashing him over and over.

She'd had months to come to terms with this. He had minutes. And he didn't dare make a mistake.

"The Caribbean. Saint Thomas has a good hospital in case I needed one. I rented a villa on the beach." Her voice wavered. "I was trying to be discreet. To keep this out of the press and away from the old family drama until I spoke to you and we could figure out how to handle the future. But just when I had everything set and was ready to call you, I went into labor three weeks early."

Now that knocked the wind out of his rising anger.

"Is he okay? Are you?" A stab of fear jabbed Jean-Pierre hard, outweighing every other emotion. His brother's wife, Fiona, had lost a baby. He understood the danger.

"We're fine. Thirty-seven weeks is within normal range. César was six pounds and fourteen ounces."

The pain in his chest eased, a small sliver of the tension giving way to an unexpected tenderness.

"César," he repeated, gaze shifting to the squirming blanket and restless tiny foot.

"For your great-grandfather and for my—"

"Grandfather," he interrupted, knowing they both had Césars in their family trees. He remembered the roots of the Doucet family almost as well as his own. He'd been a guest at their home when he'd dated Tatiana, before his grandfather Leon had fired Jack from the Texas Mustangs after two seasons of poorly performing teams.

An old bitterness that would have to take a backseat now.

"Our son is five weeks old. We just flew in from Saint Thomas two days ago. His nanny, Lucinda, made the trip with me. She watched him tonight while I went to find you."

That must have been the woman he'd seen earlier.

"May I see him?" Jean-Pierre didn't want to interrupt a feeding, but the urgency of the infant's small suckling sounds had slowed from when he'd first entered the room.

"Of course." Tatiana shifted the bundle in her arms. She lifted the baby upright, her dress falling closed. "Here's a cloth." She nodded to a square of white cotton folded beside her on the love seat. "For your shoulder if you want to—"

She trailed off as he took the baby, who was possibly quieted by Jean-Pierre's sure grip. At least half the Gladiators had kids, so he'd handled plenty during private team events. But holding this one…

"He has the Reynaud eyes." They were brown and flecked with green. The tiny hands were covered by the sleeves of his shirt, the fabric folded over them. But the boy's color was good—pink and healthy. A thatch of dark hair, spiky but soft, stood on end as if he'd been caught in a wind tunnel.

"I was only with you last year, no one else," Tatiana said softly, her dark curls brushing Jean-Pierre's shoulder as she leaned closer to look down at the infant. "He is yours."

"No question." He trusted this implicitly. He might not be happy with her decision to keep the news of her pregnancy to herself—and he was shoving aside a whole lot of unhappiness about that, in fact—yet he knew her well enough to know that she was careful with relationships.

"May I?" She reached for César. "Just to finish the feeding?"

Wordlessly, he passed the baby back to her. He watched as she slipped her dress off her other shoulder, vaguely aware that many women preferred privacy for such a moment. But he'd been denied too much time already, so he didn't take his eyes off her as she cradled the tiny body to her swollen breast and helped him to find the dark pink nipple.

"You look so…" *Beautiful*, he thought. But the moment was too intimate already with them sitting almost shoulder-to-shoulder, her curls still clinging to the sleeve of his jacket. "At ease with him."

He envied that, he realized.

"I've had more time with him." She bit her lip, perhaps guessing how that statement might sting. When she turned to face him, her eyes shone with unshed tears. "No one warned me what an emotional time this would be." She lifted a shaky hand to first one eye and then the other. "I knew pregnancy hormones could make women emotional, but I didn't count on feeling so different after giving birth. You know I'm not the kind of person to make unguarded comments to the media, and yet tonight I was so nervous about seeing you and telling you, that I just blurted that remark with zero thought."

As troubling as that seemed to be for Tatiana, it explained a whole lot of things as far as he was concerned.

"Having lived through puberty, I can assure you that I understand hormones are a powerful force of nature."

She gave a watery chuckle. "I've made a good living on being rational. Logical. It's like I'm operating on a whole new kind of software."

She gestured to the handful of baby items strewn on the coffee table—a half-open diaper bag with the contents spilling out, a stack of newspapers and some folded sheets. Not a mess by any stretch, but for a woman who liked to show a perfect face to the world, the scene probably bordered on chaos.

"Maybe that's why biology let men off the hook during pregnancy. So we can be the logical ones." He forced a grin, trying to keep things light since it wasn't going to do either of them any good to have a big confrontation about the ethics of keeping him in the dark about the pregnancy.

She'd been nervous to tell him. And he had to take some blame for that given the way he'd left things between them last winter.

"*You're* going to be the voice of reason?" She arched an eyebrow, her voice steady and full of attitude.

That was more like it.

"Definitely."

"Don't forget I was in your backyard the summer you decided it was a good idea to jump off a second-story deck into your family's pool." A smile transformed her features as she shifted her gaze down to the baby in her arms.

And it damn near took his breath away. No wonder she'd looked so good tonight. She had that new-mother glow.

"A minor sprain was a small price to pay for the serious rotation I got on that dive." He needed her smiling. Relaxed.

Trusting him.

Because he'd been formulating plans from the moment he understood the magnitude of the secret she'd been keeping.

"Nevertheless, I think I'll keep my own counsel even while I'm under the influence of my hormones."

"Fair enough. But because you're a reasonable woman, I know you're going to agree with me on this first order of business." He reached to touch her arm where she cradled their son, needing a connection with her when he made his appeal.

"We need to tell our families." Her gaze met his, the firelight reflected in their depths.

She was a beautiful woman. An intelligent, hardworking woman. And there was undeniable chemistry between them or this situation wouldn't have arisen in the first place.

"That's the second order of business." They'd take care of that soon enough. "First, we need to get married."

There was a unique brand of hurt in hearing a man you once cared about offer a sham marriage when he no longer cared about you.

Tatiana breathed through that hurt now, telling herself she could not afford to be any more emotional tonight than she already had been. But heaven help her, how could she not feel vulnerable when her arms were full of the precious baby they'd created, César's soft breath warming her breast as he began to nod off after his feeding? She was exposed in every possible way, and maybe just for a moment she'd allowed herself to sink into the warmth of Jean-Pierre beside her as they'd marveled together at their tiny shared miracle.

Carefully, she lifted the baby to her shoulder and tucked her breast back into her dress. Patting his back, she took comfort in the ritual, grounding herself in the actions of a new mother. She needed to be strong for her son, no matter that Jean-Pierre's halfhearted suggestion called to old feelings inside her. She would tamp down those emotions right now.

"The last time we met, you told me in no uncertain terms that the mistake of us being together would never be repeated." Grateful her voice didn't quaver while uttering those damning words that had caused her no end of grief these past months, she straightened to face him. "Let's not fool ourselves into thinking we can take a relationship from that level of animosity to marriage, no matter how cold-bloodedly we approach our goals. You may be a master strategist on the football field, but César and I are not components of an offense to be moved around at your will."

Jean-Pierre cocked an eyebrow. "So I assume that's a *no* to my proposal?"

Swallowing hard, she nodded. "Most definitely."

"I'm going to ask again."

"And I'm going to ask you to leave if you don't respect my wishes," she said firmly, praying he wouldn't roll out his old charm, which could too easily whittle away her shaky resistance.

"Fair enough then. For now. Because I very much want to stay. May I take him?" Jean-Pierre offered, already reaching to lift César from her shoulder. "You must be exhausted."

She wanted to argue since it comforted her to feel the baby's warm body against hers, but she was indeed tired. And she couldn't begrudge César's father this time with him. Not when he'd been denied five weeks of his life already.

"Thank you." She straightened the spit cloth that he'd tossed over his suit jacket, trying not to notice the attractive vision this powerful man made while holding his son— their child—with such tenderness. "While it's tempting to hold him all the time, I'm learning to rest more often. I was so tired the whole first week."

"I wish I'd been there to help you," he said simply. "Parenting is a team sport." He patted the baby twice, elicited the necessary burp, then tucked the infant in the crook of his arm as securely as he carried a football for a first down. "That's why I stand by the marriage offer. I don't call that cold-blooded. I call it keeping your eye on the end zone. It would benefit our son for us to work together."

"I don't think a child gains anything from parents who aren't happy and yet force themselves to be together. We'd be better off trying to figure out how to effectively co-parent." Feeling rumpled and flustered, she fastened her dress. What woman wanted to field a marriage proposal over the head of a newborn, her breasts sore and her body bone-weary from the physical odyssey of a first pregnancy?

She knew it was foolish to care, but she could only imagine how she looked right now. And yes, she wished she could have met Jean-Pierre in one of her sleek Stella McCartney dresses, but they were all still too small for her postpartum body to fit into.

"I'm not sure your father is going to think much of a plan to co-parent from separate homes." He wrapped a dangling swath of blanket around the baby's foot.

"My father also parented his football players more than his own daughter, so I'm not accepting advice on the subject from Jack Doucet." She loved her father, but she'd witnessed the way he indulged the elite athletes, giving them preferential treatment. As a teen, it had hurt to see him spend more time with them, showing up at a college prospect's house on the weekend to establish a relationship while blowing off Tatiana's debate championship—or any other noteworthy accomplishment.

Although, even as she said it, she realized that Jean-Pierre might bear more of her father's disappointment than she would. But she'd learned long ago she couldn't make decisions to please other people. She relied on herself and no one else.

"Of course." He agreed more easily than she'd expected.

"This is a lot for both of us to take in right now. We'll talk tomorrow. I can put him to bed for you if you want to get some sleep." He laid a hand over hers, a tender gesture that stirred all those emotions she couldn't control lately.

But no matter how kindly he offered help now, she couldn't forget that he'd walked away from her last time. Underneath the civil politeness, he was still the same athlete who'd spent weeks fuming silently at her while she'd methodically proved his former teammate guilty of sexual harassment. Afterward, he had continued to defend the man. If not for the spike of attraction that had never been too far beneath the surface with them, she and Jean-Pierre didn't have anything in common.

Except now they shared responsibility for this precious life they'd created.

"I have a night nurse. She can take him. She knows his routine." She glanced into Jean-Pierre's eyes quickly. "I'm sorry. You can do it soon, but please, can we keep things simple for tonight? We have so much to sort through."

Sliding her hand out from under his, Tatiana reached to take the baby, more exhausted now than she had been after eighteen hours of labor. She hadn't known how stressful speaking to Jean-Pierre would be.

But now that he finally knew the truth, some of that weight had been shifted off her shoulders.

"I'm sure the night nurse is great." He didn't hand over the sleeping infant. "But since I have lost weeks I'll never recover with him, I would appreciate being able to put him in his bed for the night."

The cool words didn't hide his judgment of her—he blamed her for not coming to him sooner about the pregnancy.

"Follow me." Too weary to argue, she rose to her feet, gladly leaving behind the gorgeous Louboutin heels. The shoes that once brought her so much joy were now instruments of torture.

She led the way up the curving staircase of her apartment, a prewar building with plenty of amenities for children that she would be taking advantage of now that she could share the news of her baby with the world.

"Should you be climbing so many stairs?" He was beside her suddenly, his hand on her lower back.

It was a warm touch despite his frustration with her.

"Stairs are fine. I didn't have a C-section so I'm in good shape." Figuratively speaking. Her actual shape still leaned toward the soft side.

"I hope you are taking care of yourself." His touch fell away as they arrived on the second floor and she pointed the way to César's room.

The night nurse greeted her as they entered the nursery, but discreetly retreated to her own bedroom across the hall.

"I am. I'm looking forward to bringing him out in the stroller for walks once we speak to my family. The fresh air will be good for both of us." Leaning into the antique crib she'd bought online and had shipped to the house before she'd even returned from the Caribbean, Tatiana slid aside the blue baby blanket. It went with the aquatic theme of the room.

She'd need major amounts of fresh air after speaking to her father. He'd always set the bar so damn high for her. Even when she was soaring at the top of her class or making junior partner ahead of schedule at her firm, she felt the pressure of his expectations. Now? She couldn't even imagine telling him that his first grandson was a Reynaud.

"We can see your parents first thing in the morning. But I would like to leave for New Orleans shortly afterward." He bent into the crib and laid César beside a stuffed baby whale.

One broad shoulder brushed the starfish mobile as he straightened, setting off a few gentle musical notes.

"You're going there to tell your family?" She knew his parents, Theo and Alessandra Reynaud, had been divorced for years and weren't even full-time residents of Louisiana anymore. Alessandra worked in Hollywood. Theo globe-hopped, content to live off his family's money. But Jean-Pierre's grandfather, Leon, still acted as the Reynaud patriarch in the public eye.

Leon, who had fired Tatiana's father from the Mustangs and created the Doucet-Reynaud rift. Her stomach clenched at the thought of facing him.

"My family can wait." Jean-Pierre stared down at her in the soft blue glow of the nursery's night-light, his strong male presence radiating warmth and making her realize how close they stood. "We need to go there together to fulfill the promise I made in a televised interview this evening. I told the world you were going to be a guest of the Reynauds before the Gladiators-Hurricanes game."

The words didn't make sense at first. He couldn't be serious about them simply pretending to be dating.

"I don't understand. Now you must see that's impossible." She gestured to the crib, where César clutched a handful of blanket. "I can't leave New York."

"We are a family now, Tatiana, whether you want to be or not." His voice suggested a patience that his body language did not. He loomed over her, tense and unyielding. "It makes more sense than ever that you come to Louisiana with me while we work out some logistics of parenting."

Her gaze slipped back down to César, peaceful and unaware of the tension between his parents. She knew that Jean-Pierre was right. They had to find some way to raise their child together even though there would be no

wedding. No pretend romance to mask the animosity between them.

Maybe, given some time, she could negotiate a peaceful
future for her son in the same way she argued court cases.
She would find a way to get on top of her runaway pregnancy hormones and the mixed feelings she still had for
Jean-Pierre—hurt, resentment, attraction. A potent mix.

"I'll need a private room," she said finally, tilting her
chin up and laying the groundwork for this very dicey
compromise. "I will go with you, but I can't perform a
charade for the media or our families."

"Meaning you won't pretend to like the father of your
child?" One heavy eyebrow arched as he watched her.

Her heartbeat quickened for no discernible reason. They
were drawing boundaries, weren't they? That was a good
thing.

"Meaning there will be no maneuvering each other by
implying an engagement or imminent wedding that we
both know will not happen."

"Deal." His agreement was quick and easy, catching her
off guard. He took her hand in his. "You have my word."

His touch sparked memories of another time they'd been
face-to-face like this—arguing heatedly about her court
case. He'd touched her to emphasize a point, perhaps. And
somewhere in that moment, the chemistry of the contact
had shifted, turning heated. Making it impossible to pull
their hands off of each other. She felt the weight of that
moment now, along with the possibility that it could happen again if she wasn't careful. It was there, in her flut-
tering pulse. In her rapid breathing.

She hovered there, on that razor's edge between tension
and attraction, understanding too late how easy it would
be to slide into that dangerous terrain.

"Sleep well then." He lifted her hand to his lips. Brushed

a brief kiss along the backs of her fingers as though it was the most natural thing in the world. "I'll pick you up in the morning so we can speak to your father together. And make no mistake, I will be there by your side."

She nodded, her mouth dry, her skin tingling where he'd kissed her. She watched Jean-Pierre turn to leave and show himself out, her emotions tangled, knotted and taut. She had thought telling him about their child would be the most difficult thing she'd ever have to do. But now, feeling the way her body still responded to him, she knew that resisting the lure of a Reynaud man would be a challenge beyond anything she'd imagined.

Three

Between NFL games, Jean-Pierre had a week to strategize. He studied his opponent, searching for weaknesses and ways to exploit them. He developed a game plan and made adjustments right up until the moment when he took the field to execute it.

With Tatiana, he didn't have a week for anything.

He'd had twelve intense hours to get his head around fatherhood before facing her family with news that had obviously blindsided them. Twelve hours to figure out his game plan, when his whole world was off balance. And while they'd delivered the news to the Doucets in their living room half an hour ago and it had gone as smoothly as could be expected, Jean-Pierre now braced himself for whatever his coach wanted to say to him privately. In a room nearby, the women took turns holding César while he watched Jack Doucet shut the door behind him and turn on him.

"You bastard." Red-faced, his coach stared him down with a fury he no longer hid. A defensive end in his college days, Jack had softened in his coaching years, a rounded gut and flushed face attesting to the comfortable life of a man who didn't deny himself any pleasures.

But right now, with the look in the older man's eye, Jean-Pierre didn't doubt for a second the guy would deliver one hell of a hit if he decided to come after him.

"She didn't tell me," Jean-Pierre reminded him, remembering the time the coach had hurled a helmet across the locker room into a rookie's head for missing his play cue. "I didn't know until last night and I'm here now—"

"Don't bullshit me. A man always knows there's a chance." Jack's fists clenched at his sides, his chin jutting closer. "That's my daughter we're talking about."

"And that's my son." Jean-Pierre kept his voice quiet, recognizing the imperative of keeping a lid on this conversation with the women in the other room. "And since we both want to protect our families, I suggest we figure out how to have this discussion without upsetting anyone on the other side of that door." His heart slugged hard in his chest.

He did not want a brawl to commemorate this day. That wasn't the kind of start he needed with Tatiana.

"As much as I'd like to plant my fist in your jaw, even if it cost you a game, Reynaud, you have a point." The older man spun on his heel and turned to the bar. He poured himself a measure of Irish whiskey from a bottle centered on a silver serving tray.

Jean-Pierre hoped the whiskey cooled him off. He edged back a step, waiting to resume their conversation once Jack had a hold of himself.

All around the study were framed news clippings and photographs from Jack's career as a head coach in New

York. The most prominent photos were of the team's two division championships and a Super Bowl win four years ago. There were no photos from Jack's years as Leon Reynaud's second in command for the Mustangs, even though the two of them had taken the team to new heights, developing a fast style of offense copied throughout the league and setting records in passing that still stood today.

Jack had severed all ties with Leon and the Reynauds until he needed a strong quarterback to lead the Gladiators. Even then, the head coach hadn't done much to make Jean-Pierre feel welcome in New York. They'd simply worked toward their common goal to make the Gladiators a powerhouse team again.

"You've got a hell of a lot of nerve." Jack slammed the whiskey glass on the desk as he turned to face him. "I brought you to New York to give you a chance to step out of the family shadow. To make your own mark on this game. And this is how you repay me?" He gripped the neck of the whiskey bottle tighter, his voice low.

"Now I'd like to return the favor and ask that you don't try to bullshit me. You didn't bring me here out of the kindness of your heart. You brought me here to win games," he said evenly. "I've done that and more."

Jack remained silent as he scrubbed a hand through thinning hair.

"I've played my part for you," Jean-Pierre continued. "A little too damn well now that I think about it. It's one thing for you to ask me to win games, but it was another to expect me to stay away from Tatiana."

He'd backed off ten years ago when she had sided with her family and told him they were through. But all those old feelings hadn't just evaporated because Jack Doucet told his daughter not to see him anymore. They'd been festering somewhere inside them both, only to implode that day in the courtroom when he'd confronted her after the case.

"I should have never brought you to the Gladiators," Jack muttered, pouring himself a third shot.

"Beyond the winning record, I've provided the locker-room stability you need to keep a team of aging veterans and wild rookies on the same page each week. If you're unhappy with my performance, I'm happy to revisit our terms at contract time." Knowing he wasn't going to smooth over this problem today, he wondered how soon he could reasonably walk out of the Doucet household with Tatiana and his son.

His son.

He still couldn't think about the magnitude of that news without the words reverberating through him long afterward. But he needed to move past the awe of it fast in order to protect César's future. He had so much to organize, so many plans to put in place. Not the least of which was convincing Tatiana to stay with him.

It was a feat that he'd never achieve while her father remained furious with him. But dammit, he needed to ensure César had the kind of stability his own life had lacked. Theo's illegitimate son—Jean-Pierre's half brother, Dempsey—had suffered the consequences of their father's choices his whole life. Jean-Pierre didn't want that for César.

"I don't care if you set the record for completions this season." The older man raised his voice, scaring off a heavy gray tabby cat that had been snoozing on the leather chair behind the desk. The animal took cover behind a red drapery and peered down into the expansive view of Central Park. "I want my daughter happy and my grandson to have a name."

"He has my name. My protection. All the resources my

family can possibly give him." He'd been up most of the night working out details with his lawyer to ensure paperwork was already in motion.

"Let me be clearer." Jack shook a finger too damn close to Jean-Pierre's face. "I want my grandson to have a name that isn't Reynaud."

"Nevertheless, I will do everything possible to ensure Tatiana is taken care of as well. You know as well as I do that being a Reynaud ensures she'll never want for anything."

"Meaning you will marry her?" Appearing to mull this over, Jack strode over to the tabby cat, picked it up and stroked the animal's broad head.

"She asked me not to pressure her about that and I will do as she requests."

"But you will see that it happens." The coach met his gaze over the cat's head.

It was a directive, not a question. Maybe Jean-Pierre would have resisted more if he hadn't been on the same page with the man.

"That's my intent. Yes. But I'm curious. You wouldn't protest a union between families? Despite the rift?" He remembered a time when the Doucets had taken away Tatiana's car as a punishment for driving to see him.

That was a long time ago, but Jack held the kind of grudges that grew deeper with age.

"You've given me little choice."

"I have two weeks with her in New Orleans and even she won't back out of that." He wouldn't break his agreement with Tatiana by implying a union she might not agree to. But he also couldn't afford putting more pressure on the Gladiators by ticking off his coach further. "I hope that attending my brother's wedding will make her reconsider marriage."

"I'm not so sure about that plan. She ought to keep the child secret longer down there," her father mused. "Old Leon must have the family compound locked down like Fort Knox with a foreign princess on the grounds."

"It's secure. There will be no media unless Tatiana chooses to speak with reporters." He hadn't really considered that option—keeping César a secret from the press for a while longer. But maybe Jack had a point. There would be pressure enough on them with the media interest already brewing. "I won't be budging on that."

"Good." Jack set down the cat on a wingback chair. "By the time I see an announcement about my grandson in the papers, it will coincide with news of your marriage."

He didn't argue with Jack. But as he stood to exit the study with him, he couldn't help but remind him of one important fact.

"It has to be her idea to get married since she's already put her foot down on the subject." He understood that much about her. She was a strong-minded woman and she didn't budge once she made up her mind. He'd seen it in the courtroom last year.

"And so it will be." Jack opened up the door and gestured for Jean-Pierre to go ahead of him. "Because if it's not, you can start looking for a new team. I can guarantee that if I'm not happy with you, son, I'll do everything in my power to bury your career."

"I've missed this place." Tatiana stared out the window of the chauffeur-driven luxury SUV that had met them at the private airport just outside of New Orleans.

Spanish moss dripped from live oak trees on either side of the private driveway leading into the Reynaud estate on Lake Pontchartrain in an exclusive section of Metairie, Louisiana, west of the city. Pontoon boats were moored in the shallow waters while long docks stretched into the low-lying mist that had settled on the surface. The green of the gardens was rich and verdant, the ground so fertile that a team of gardeners was needed to hold back the wild undergrowth that could take over land like this in just a few short weeks' time.

She knew because her family's yard had been like that, full of kudzu back when her father had been with the Texas football team. The Doucets didn't have the same level of wealth as the Reynauds and even now, the apartments on Central Park West were relatively new luxuries. Back when Tatiana had attended prep school nearby, her mother had taken a condo in Baton Rouge while her father remained in East Texas for his job with the Mustangs.

Jean-Pierre sat beside her while César napped in his car seat in the bench-row seat ahead of them. The trip had been smooth, from the car service in New York to the quick private flight to the spacious SUV with a Reynaud family driver to load their luggage. She wished she knew what exactly had transpired between Jean-Pierre and her father when they left to speak privately, but she'd only learned that her father suggested they keep news of César out of the press for as long as possible, an approach that made sense while they figured out how to share custody.

After leaving her parents' home, Jean-Pierre had assured her that he would immediately outfit a nursery in Louisiana for César, so she hadn't brought much for him. The baby's night nurse would fly to New Orleans later, but until then, local staff had been retained to help Lucinda.

Tatiana had to admit, Jean-Pierre had made things as easy as possible for her. And while she'd guessed he would probably step up and be supportive of their child, a small part of her had feared otherwise. That he would be too angry at being shut out of César's birth to treat her with so much thoughtfulness. She'd hardly slept the night before, wondering how today would be with him, not to mention all of his family.

"I miss this city every time I'm away," he confided to her now. Leaning forward to look at the lake with her, Jean-Pierre was a warm, vital presence in the vehicle.

The tinted windows ensured their privacy as they rounded the first bend. She spotted a Greek revival mansion that hadn't been there before.

"Wow." She marveled at how well the new home complemented the existing one where Jean-Pierre had grown up, a home she'd visited as a teen even before they dated since her father had worked with Leon Reynaud. "Did Gervais build this for his soon-to-be bride?"

Speculation about Gervais and Princess Erika's wedding had filled the tabloids for weeks. Tatiana had devoured the articles during those uncomfortable last weeks of pregnancy when she had done little more than read and wait.

"No. Dempsey had this built when he took over as head coach of the Hurricanes. Gervais and Erika are in the original home." Jean-Pierre pointed to the mansion, which was almost double the size of the Greek revival house, on the other side of the street. "Henri and I share time in the big Italianate monstrosity that Leon purchased for guests when we were young. You remember it?"

"The abandoned house where you wanted to celebrate my seventeenth birthday?" Her skin warmed at the memory. She'd had such a crush on him back then, she would have followed him anywhere. Even into a house that had been fenced off and marked with construction-zone signs.

But he'd just started attending the same school as she and they'd been spending more time together. Their families had been friends for years—before the big rift—so they'd had an easy relationship marked by meetings at football games or summer homes. But once Jean-Pierre had enrolled in her school, things shifted between them. She couldn't keep her eyes off him.

That weekend at the Reynauds' house—her birthday weekend—had moved things out of the friend zone. He'd kissed her that night and everything had changed.

"You have to admit I made you one hell of a birthday cake." His gaze lingered on her. Was he thinking about that kiss, too?

"Or your family chef did." She refused to be charmed by old memories. There were too many unhappy newer ones.

"But how do you think he knew to make a raspberry almond torte with purple frosting?"

"I was in a serious purple phase."

She had all but melted at his feet when he brought it out with seventeen lit wooden matches in place of the candles he'd forgotten. They'd eaten it on the dock outside the boathouse, and she'd informed him that at seventeen, she was officially old enough to be his girlfriend.

The night had only gotten more romantic after he fed her that first piece of cake.

He'd been eighteen, worldly beyond any other boy she knew, and wary of dating someone younger. But she'd been persistent.

"Not much has changed." He gave the hem of her skirt a light tug for emphasis, the lavender silk edged with darker plum fringe.

Through the fringe, the back of one knuckle grazed her bare knee and sent a jolt of adrenaline buzzing up her thigh. She bit the inside of her cheek.

"I've only just returned to bright colors, though. For years, I draped myself in navy and beige when I went in front of a jury." She'd grown tired of the conservative wardrobe her career dictated, but she hadn't realized how much she'd reined in her fashion creativity until her more recent wardrobe choices had all been bright colors, sequins, feathers and fringe.

"Anything to win a case," he remarked dryly, no doubt thinking of the civil suit she'd won against his friend.

"I hope you don't expect me to apologize for being good at my job." They might as well address it since it had been the source of their last argument, the reason he'd walked out on her and said their time together had been a mistake. "It's not up to me to determine right from wrong. That's a jury's job. I'm simply paid to win. Just like you are."

She tucked her phone into her purse as the vehicle stopped in front of the stucco Italianate mansion that had been updated and whitewashed since the last time she'd been here. Their driver, a former Hurricanes' player named Evan, opened the back door for them and began to bring their bags inside.

"You didn't use to believe in winning at any cost." He didn't move to exit the vehicle.

"That was before I realized that if you don't fight for yourself, no one else is going to fight for you." She reached into the car seat to unbuckle César, but Jean-Pierre took over the task.

"Let me." He lifted the baby in one arm and stepped out into the sunlight to help her exit the SUV. He held onto her arm even after she stood by his side. "Do you really think I didn't fight for you all those years ago?"

She didn't need to ask what he was talking about. She'd been hurt when he hadn't tried harder to see her despite their families' dictate that they stay away from each other.

"It's ancient history now." She wasn't about to admit how much that breakup had stung.

Especially not now, when she needed to shape a future

for herself and her son. The less she looked back at the past, the better.

"I hope so. We've got a whole future ahead of us to plan." His hand found the small of her back as she stepped up onto the stone landing of the front steps. "Together."

His touch set off the familiar awareness that he'd always inspired. And how potent it felt now as they moved toward the threshold of this home with their son in his arms.

She'd be staying for two weeks inside a home where Jean-Pierre had almost seduced her ten years ago. How resistant would she be here, of all places, when they shared so much history? Lucky for her, she had César to remind her of her priorities. She wouldn't allow herself to be trapped in a loveless marriage. Children didn't thrive in that kind of stilted environment.

"I'm sure we'll figure out an equitable arrangement." Her familiarity with legal settlements had already prompted her to draw up some possible scenarios for sharing custody, but she wanted to wait a few days to raise the topic for discussion.

Give him some time to see she genuinely wanted what was best for their child.

"His happiness will be our highest priority." Jean-Pierre shifted César in his arms and the baby made a soft cooing sound. "Welcome back, Tatiana. If there's anything I can do to make your stay here more comfortable, I hope you'll let me know."

"Thank you." She felt the warm Louisiana breeze tousle her curls. Camellias and roses all around the front entrance beckoned her toward the open door. "It looks so much different."

"I should hope so. You've been gone a long time." He followed her into the cool foyer, where pale tile floors and heavy, dark furnishings gave the place a Mediterranean feel.

A courtyard ahead of them made her realize the house was built around a wide space that was open to the sunlight. Terra-cotta floors and some kind of potted citrus trees imparted a warmth to the home she hadn't expected. Brightly patterned pillows decorated carved wooden benches while a water feature in the center gurgled softly.

"It's very inviting." She could picture herself here, surrounded by sunlight and flowers.

"Fiona, Henri's wife, did some decorating when they married. But Henri and Fiona will be staying at their home in the Garden District all during the wedding festivities. So we'll have this whole place to ourselves." He gestured toward the steps and she followed him up the gently rounded staircase.

"I may need a map to navigate." She peered over the thick banister down into the foyer, noting the tapestry that bore a Reynaud family shield from the days of the Crusades. Jean-Pierre had written a paper on the meaning of the heraldry in high school and she'd proofread it for him before he turned it in.

"Hardly. Your father's house in the Hamptons is bigger than this." He pointed to a room on the left side of the main corridor upstairs and led her into a nursery decorated in gray, blue and yellow. A stuffed giraffe almost as tall as the ceiling stood in one corner, watching over the crib. A carved fireplace covered with a cream-colored grate took up the opposite wall.

While Jean-Pierre lay the still snoozing baby in the crib, she marveled at all the special details in place for the room's tiny occupant. Besides the beautiful décor, the open closet held extra blankets, diapers, towels and clothes.

A discreet changing station had been built in to the gray cabinetry.

"Your staff must have worked all night to decorate." She couldn't imagine how they'd created the beautiful space so quickly. "Are you sure we'll be able to keep César a secret if—"

"The staff here is carefully screened and sign confidentiality agreements before working with the family. But in this case, I didn't need to ask for extra help. Henri and Fiona had already installed the basics for a nursery before…" He straightened from the crib. "Fiona lost a pregnancy and they had a difficult stretch. Her experience makes me all the more grateful you and César are both healthy and thriving."

The concern in his eyes told her how deeply he meant it. The emotion she glimpsed touched her, even as her heart ached for his brother and sister-in-law.

"I can't imagine how hard that must have been." She leaned into the crib to kiss her son's soft baby hair. The mattress was raised to the highest setting inside the wooden rails since he was too young to sit up on his own.

"Thankfully, she's well now. There's a video monitoring system if you'd like to keep an eye on him." He pointed to a handheld device broadcasting a color image of the crib. "The camera is inside the giraffe's mouth. You can also program your phone to pick up the feed if that's easier for you."

"That would be great." She hugged her arms around herself, feeling oddly adrift without César to hold now that she'd handed off some of his care to Jean-Pierre. "I will rest easier knowing I can check on him without even leaving my room."

"I can introduce you to the relief caregiver later, to help out when Lucinda needs a break. I'll show you to your room first. You must be exhausted with so much travel in the last week."

Not to mention the stress of telling him about their child.

But she didn't remind him of that.

"Thank you. I would appreciate it." She tucked the nursery monitor in her bag and followed him through the wide hallway to a room two doors down.

"I thought you'd prefer to be close to César, although if the room isn't to your liking, there are several other options." He switched on a chandelier, even though daylight still shone in through the floor-to-ceiling windows on the exterior wall.

At first, she thought he'd brought her into a family room by mistake. But it was actually the sitting area of a spacious guest suite. Beyond the couches and wet bar of the living space, two steps led into the bedroom, the area divided by a low wall with two red marble pillars. A king-size bed was tucked into a corner beside an exit to a private terrace overlooking the lake. A fireplace had been built into one wall, and a ceiling fan turned languidly over the bed. The ceilings had to be at least fifteen feet high.

"The Reynauds live well," she said finally, setting her bag on one of the long, forest green couches. "I'm sure this room will be more than adequate."

"Good." He nodded, satisfied. "I told Evan to put your luggage in the closet, but I can send someone up to unpack for you."

"That's not necessary." She'd forgotten the level of wealth in his family. The Reynauds didn't just have homes around the globe. They had well-staffed homes. Private planes. A global shipping empire.

For her father, football was a lucrative career. For the Reynauds, it was a passion and a pastime, the income a small facet of a net worth she couldn't fully appreciate. And while that was all very nice for them, she wasn't sure how she felt about having her son raised to think this was how people lived.

"As you wish." He nodded and backed up a step. "Dinner is at seven thirty if you'd like to rest before then. The caregiver can oversee César's next feeding if Lucinda needs to unpack."

"No." She wouldn't hand over her son to a woman she hadn't even met yet. "I'll just keep the monitor close by." She retrieved it from her bag.

"But you'll join me for dinner?" he asked. He did not demand. "I've asked my family to give us some privacy until we settle in, so it will be just us tonight."

She appreciated that for a lot of reasons, not the least of which was needing to steel herself for a reunion with a family she hadn't acknowledged in a decade. A family that had been kind to her, whose kindness she'd repaid by turning her back on them when her father told her to.

But she was also glad for the way Jean-Pierre seemed to understand she needed some time and space to make her own decision about their future together. She was grateful for that right now when she was beginning to feel overwhelmed by this life of privilege.

"Dinner sounds nice." Maybe after a shower and a change of clothes she'd feel less vulnerable, more ready to stake her claim for a future independent of Reynaud influence. "I look forward to it."

She said it as a polite social nicety. But something flared in his eyes at the words, a heated interest she didn't miss. That he could feel attracted to her now—when she was bone-weary and still recovering from pregnancy—caught her by surprise. It amazed her even more to realize his interest stirred her own.

Where would he be sleeping? And what a crazy thought that was on more than one level. The doctor hadn't even cleared her for sex yet. If she was even planning on having sex with Jean-Pierre again. Which she wasn't.

"As do I." His gaze roamed over her, warming every place it rested. "Until then, you should feel safe to walk the grounds if you wish. Between the extra security on staff for the wedding and the usual precautions around the property, you won't have to worry about any unwelcome interruptions from the media. Just be careful near the lake or on the decks overlooking the water. Telephoto lenses from boats or nearby properties would be able to capture images at that distance."

"I'll keep that in mind." She would keep her blinds closed as well, as much as she'd prefer the water view. "The longer we can protect César's privacy, the better. Although some photos of you and me here together might help quiet the rumors I created back in New York."

"If you feel up for a boat ride tomorrow, I'll take you out on the lake." His gaze held hers. "Just like old times."

A half smile teased his mouth as he reached for the door. A shared memory flashed between them. He used to take her out on the boat to be alone with her—away from his family. They would anchor near a quiet cove and steal belowdecks. She would try to tempt him enough to forget the restraints he'd always put on their relationship, always knowing she was safe with him. But there were times that they'd pushed the boundaries...

Just thinking about those trips warmed her skin. The urge to kiss him flared hot even though they stood on opposite sides of the room. She licked her lips instead, suddenly nervous.

"I'm sorry you have to spend your time staging photo opportunities for the press to cover up my mistake with that reporter." She had never understood how he could rattle her so easily when she felt sure of herself with the rest of the world.

His hand fell away from the door but he didn't advance toward her.

"Even if it hadn't been for that comment to the reporter, we would need to be together this week anyway." The hint of a smile had vanished, his expression serious. "You and César are my highest priorities now."

Jean-Pierre would bear his responsibilities because he had to, not because he wanted to. She nodded, understanding better than he realized.

As he left her alone to rest and unpack, Tatiana knew it would be a stretch to appear in photos with him as if they were still old friends. The truth was that they were so much more than that. Enemies, lovers, parents. A combustible combination with attraction simmering just below the surface.

It would take a whole lot of focus just to keep it from boiling over.

Four

"Tatiana?"

A man's voice awoke her later that night, the sultry drawl of a Cajun accent lingering in her ear. Confused about the time and her whereabouts, she struggled to orient herself. A strange coverlet pressed into her cheek, the pale piping making a ridge along her jaw. Moonlight streamed in through a door near her bed where she'd forgotten to close the blinds. She lay atop the duvet, still fully clothed.

"Jean-Pierre?" The voice sounded so close to her, but she didn't see him in the moonlit room.

Had she been dreaming of him?

"I'm in César's room," the voice returned softly, the sound coming through the nursery monitor, which rested on the bed nearby. "I wasn't sure if you heard him cry, but I think he's hungry if you still want to feed him."

Waking faster now, she realized it must be late. Her breasts were swollen to aching.

"Yes. I'm coming." She scrambled off the bed, wishing she'd changed into something more comfortable. She was a wrinkled mess in her traveling clothes. She must have slept right through dinner.

"Don't hurry. We're fine." The gentleness in Jean-Pierre's tone slipped right past her boundaries, making her smile. Of course, the warmth and kindness were intended for his son. He was speaking as much to César as to her. "It's a nice night if you want to sit outside. I've got a fire going."

"I'd like that." Her eye went to the door; she could see a blaze in one of the fire pits. She hurried anyway, thinking maybe she had time to slide into fresh clothes after all.

"I'll stop by the kitchen to grab you something to eat. You must be hungry," he said as she slid out of her dress and into a pair of knit pajama pants and a matching button-up top that made nursing easier.

Hearing him while she was mostly naked roused a whole host of feelings she wasn't ready to deal with.

"I'm on my way." She grabbed a throw blanket off the end of the bed for good measure. The more barriers between her and Jean-Pierre, the better.

She had to remind herself that he only saw her as a responsibility. A duty to be handled, the way he competently managed every other task and obstacle life had thrown his way.

Steeling herself with that chilling reminder, she ventured out onto the second-floor veranda.

The cool breeze carried the scent of wood smoke and ginger. The gardens here were heavy with flowers even though it was November. Camellias bloomed all around, along with a golden flower on nearby trees she didn't recognize. But the fragrant ginger came from dense plantings of white flowers lining the paths around the pool. She'd noticed it earlier as she was falling asleep, the Louisiana breezes taking her back to childhood and happier times when her father had worked with Leon Reynaud and the families had spring holidays here after the football season ended.

"Someone misses you," Jean-Pierre called to her from a spot by the fire.

Rounding a hedgerow on the far side of the pool, she spotted the Adirondack chairs pulled up to a round fire pit surrounded by a low wall of flat rocks. A glider swing with a seat as big as a full-size bed anchored the space, draped in breezy white gauze threaded with a few fairy lights overhead. The cushion in the swing was draped in colorful blankets, as if someone had dragged half the contents of the linen closet outdoors.

"I think I see my seat." She hugged the blanket she was carrying like a shawl, tightening it around her as she stepped into the firelight.

Jean-Pierre rose from one of the chairs. César was wide-eyed in his arms, their son's tiny face only half visible behind his father's shoulder. Even in his casual clothes, Jean-Pierre looked crisp and pressed while she felt rumpled and tired from the long nap she hadn't meant to take.

The stress of the last weeks must have caught up to her.

"I didn't know how cold it might be when I first came out here, so I loaded up on the blankets." He followed her as she made herself comfortable in the glider swing, the cushion so thick a small child could use it as a trampoline.

"You were trying to lure me outside?" She covered her legs with one of the extrasoft wooly throws even though the fire warmed the area just fine.

The blaze crackled as a log shifted.

"I thought the view out here would be nicer than in the nursery." He dragged another pillow over from the other end of the swing and tucked it between her hip and the arm of the swing. "The whole reason Leon bought this property was for the view. If not for the lake, we'd be in the Garden District."

"It would be tougher to create a Reynaud compound in a city where families hold on to their houses for centuries." She loved the Garden District, but she guessed it would be difficult to find homes close together up for sale at the same time.

Here, the Reynauds had three homes and plenty of lake frontage.

"Leon was smart to think about privacy." Jean-Pierre didn't hand her the baby yet, instead gesturing toward a server holding a small tray that Tatiana hadn't noticed. "It's easier to keep the media at bay here."

The young woman flicked open a silver stand with one hand and settled the tray on top of it with the other, never so much as wobbling the full urn of ice water or the pot of tea wrapped in a bright red cozy. The food was hidden beneath gleaming domes that she didn't take off before hurrying away.

"This is what you meant when you said you were going to stop by the kitchen for something to eat?" Tatiana reached for César as soon as the server left.

"I might be new to child-rearing, but I figured it was best not to juggle the pot of tea while carrying a newborn." He passed the baby over, carefully supporting his head until she had him secured.

Already, the baby arched and squirmed, making small hungry sounds until she settled him to her breast. He latched on with the fierceness of an experienced eater.

"Here." Jean-Pierre folded one of the extra blankets and tucked it under her arm where the baby's head rested. "Does that help?"

"Definitely." She'd never been so comfortable while nursing, in fact. "This is an incredible setup. I wish all the nighttime feedings had been this easy."

His jaw flexed, the muscle working as he leaned over to pull the lids off the food trays. "All future feedings can be."

"Although this week, you have a light schedule with football. Normally, you'd be working." She kept her focus on the fruit-and-cheese board he'd revealed, not wanting to launch into an argument with him. But she refused to let him paint a false picture of the role he could play in any kind of family life.

She picked up a slice of kiwi and popped it into her mouth.

"I don't work at this hour." He used a pair of tongs to transfer select pieces of fruit and cheese to a smaller plate.

"But if you're on the road, that's as good as working since you wouldn't be at home," the lawyer in her pointed out, unable to resist.

He set the painted china dish on the glider cushion near César's feet, putting it in easy reach. His arm brushed hers, a warm, solid weight that had her wondering what it would be like to lean on him. Into him.

She took a piece of crusty bread and bit into it.

"Other players' families travel with them to have more time together." He loaded a second plate for himself, pulling items from another tray of cold meats.

Seeing him balance salmon and chicken on the too-small plate made her remember how careful he was about what he ate. Other players—big, heavy lineman or younger men new to the league—might see their job as a ticket to eat as much as they wanted. But even as a teen, Jean-Pierre had made a study of nutrition and workouts, turning his body into a lean, muscular machine uniquely adapted for the quarterback role. He swore the good diet and fitness regimen minimized injuries and would keep him playing longer.

Yet another way he opted to forego pleasure for obligation, dutifully doing the right thing.

"Maybe some families sacrifice one spouse's career for the sake of the other's." She helped herself to a strawberry, grateful her job didn't call for her to choke down extra protein at all hours of the day. "But I'm not sure how happy that makes everyone in the long run. Not to mention the hardship on the children. That's a lot of moving around."

"Did you mind being on the road during the season as a kid?" Finished loading up his plate, he tugged an Adirondack chair closer to the glider and sat down.

"Loaded question." During the football season, she was able to spend more time with her father, but that came with its own set of challenges. She stared into the flames as she stroked the soft tuft of hair on César's head. His suckling had slowed, reminding her she should move him to the other side to nurse.

"You loved it and so did I. What's loaded about that?"

"We were overprivileged, with way too much freedom." She didn't want to raise her son like that. "Our parents didn't keep track of us half the time and we could have gotten into all kinds of trouble."

"But we didn't. And we learned self-sufficiency."

Lifting up César, she laid him against her shoulder and patted his back.

"Having kids learn through trial by fire isn't my idea of good parenting." Even though she got the most time with her father during football season, he still seemed happiest with her when she amused herself all day and stayed out of his hair so he could focus on his duties with the Texas team.

If that meant she made a game of seeing how long she

could leave the hotel without anyone noticing she was gone, her father praised her—days later, of course—for how "good" she'd been during the week.

"But you can be an effective parent whether you're at home or not. My point is, kids are adaptable. They don't need to be in the same house day in and day out to feel a sense of stability. That comes from family, not a place." He worked methodically through his food and through his argument.

The lawyer in her should appreciate the well-reasoned views, at least. But it frustrated her that this man, of all people, didn't understand her better than that.

He'd been a part of her past. He'd seen her father in action.

"All the more reason why it's important to build a functional, loving family and not a group bound by duty alone." She shifted the baby to the other side and Jean-Pierre reached to reorganize her plate, her pillow and the prop under César's head.

"Being dutiful means being committed. Some people would think that's a good thing in a family relationship. Devotion and commitment are important components of stability." He even tugged the blanket back over her toes after it had gotten tangled from all the movement.

She had to appreciate his thoughtfulness. But his carefully scripted sense of family? It sounded like a pale imitation of the kind of loving relationship she'd once dreamed about.

"I'm sure César will benefit from those qualities." There was a cool breeze carrying the dampness of the lake, so she wrapped the baby blanket tighter around him. "I'm anxious to work out a way to co-parent, too, believe me. But it's been a long day and maybe we should table the rest of this discussion until tomorrow when I'm more clearheaded."

"You mean after you've had time to prepare your open-ing arguments?" He rose from his seat and paced the patio around the fire pit, one hand shoved in his pocket.

"No." She shook her head, wearier than ever despite the nap. "After I've caught up on some rest. I didn't ex-pect motherhood to be so exhausting and I think the added stress of knowing we needed to work out so much be-tween us had been weighing on me more than I realized. Now, it's like all the stress of the last few months has just drained me."

He quit pacing.

"Of course." His nod was sympathetic. Dutiful. "May I take him from you? I'd appreciate the chance to put him back in his crib and tuck him in for the night."

Ah, that wasn't just duty, though. She could hear the emotion behind the words, no matter how drily they were delivered.

"Certainly. Thank you." She wished, just for a mo-ment, that he was tucking her in, too. Blinking fast, she ignored the wayward thought and passed César to his fa-ther. Jean-Pierre took him in one arm. With his other hand, he reached toward her, gently pulling her blouse back into place over her half-bared breast.

Her eyes flew to his. Held.

"Thank you, Tatiana, for taking good care of him." Jean-Pierre covered the baby's back with his broad hand and patted gently. "I hope we can learn to be friends again somehow. For his sake, we will need to trust each other."

"We will." She had to believe that. She loved her new-born son. There was no other option than to find a way through this mess she'd made in not letting Jean-Pierre know sooner. "Tonight was a start for the three of us. Hav-ing you with me allowed me to catch up on some much-needed rest. Tomorrow, we'll figure out our next steps."

"A boat ride is good for clearing the head." He extended a hand to her. "Can I walk you back to your room?"

"If you don't mind, I think I'll watch the stars a little longer and have a cup of the tea." She needed to give herself a mental pep talk before his family descended on them tomorrow. Before that boat ride that he'd promised.

The excursion wouldn't include César, so she wouldn't have her son's warm weight in her arms, reminding her to tread carefully with Jean-Pierre.

"I'll be glad to know you're down here enjoying some quiet time." He brushed a touch along her cheek, stirring her curls and her awareness. "We could make one hell of a team, Tatiana."

For a moment, she wanted to tell him that their time to figure that out had passed. That they'd had a chance to be together long ago and lost it. Twice. First when they caved to family pressure to split up. Again when they settled a heated disagreement with sex instead of talking.

But she couldn't end the night on a sad note. He was trying, after all. And he would make a great father for César. But after the way he'd walked out on her ten months ago, he simply would never be more than that to her.

"Care to tell me why I have to read the papers to find out my kid brother is in town?"

Straightening from his work on the midsize power yacht he'd towed out of the boathouse, Jean-Pierre squinted into the morning sunlight to see Dempsey on the dock.

As the New Orleans Hurricanes head coach, Dempsey was the public face of the team owned by their older brother, Gervais. All too soon, they'd be standing on opposite sides of the football field inside the Zephyr Dome, pitted against each other in the matchup that had both the local and national sports media talking.

"You knew damn well I'd be coming down here to steal a firsthand look at your playbook." Jean-Pierre strode across the bow toward the back of the boat as Dempsey stepped aboard. "Good to see you, bro." He threw a few air punches at him by way of greeting.

Dempsey clapped him on the shoulder. "You're supposed to be here for a wedding, not work."

"That, too." Jean-Pierre returned to fixing the trim on a fishing-rod holder that had snapped while the boat was in storage. "Have a seat. Tell me what's new."

"How about *you* tell *me*? Sounds like this thing with Tatiana Doucet is new." Dempsey slid into the captain's seat and went to work checking the electrical components for him, systematically flipping switches and looking below the bridge area at the wiring.

Dempsey was good like that. Technically his half brother, Dempsey had been raised until he was thirteen without knowing who his real father was, so he didn't have the same upbringing as the rest of the Reynauds. For thirteen years he'd taken care of his drug-addicted mother, getting by on a meal or two a day. And while he lived a far more extravagant lifestyle now, he'd never really shaken that complete self-reliance. And his ability to fix things with his own two hands was legendary.

Although right now, Jean-Pierre sincerely hoped he wasn't the target for his brother's next fix-it-up project.

"You can't blame me for trying to spin a story for the press after she threw me under the bus with that comment about not betting against Henri for our matchup." He understood now why she'd said it. She'd been nervous about seeing him and overtired from caring for a newborn.

It still stung that she'd said it. The way it still stung that she hadn't told him she was pregnant months ago.

He twisted a nut tighter with his vise grips, his teeth grinding in frustration.

"I get it. I've been known to use the media to my advantage in the past." Dempsey thumbed through the open tool kit on the deck and pulled out a volt meter. "When I didn't want Adelaide to quit her job as my personal assistant, I announced our engagement."

Jean-Pierre put down the vise grips and stared at his brother. "Seriously? I thought you two were crazy about each other."

"That came later." Dempsey used the volt meter to test the battery and tossed it back in the tool kit. "And it wasn't easy for her that I put her on the spot like that."

"It worked, though. You're engaged for real now, aren't you?" He wondered how well he knew his brother after all.

"Damn straight. But I can tell you it wasn't as easy as me saying it was so. Women expect a lot more than that."

And men expected to be informed of impending fatherhood. But clearly he and Tatiana were making this up as they went along.

"I know smoothing things out with Tatiana isn't going to be easy, either." He debated how much to say on the subject and then decided to go for broke. "She left town this summer and I didn't know why until two nights ago. She gave birth to our son without telling anyone. Not even her family."

Dempsey's eyes widened for a split second before he could school his features. "You weren't there with her when your boy was born?"

Jean-Pierre tensed at the accusation in his brother's tone.

"I didn't even know about him. She never told me she was pregnant." Jean-Pierre could hear the frustration in his own voice; he sure hadn't expected to have to defend himself to his own family.

"You weren't in a relationship?"

"Correct."

"You're damn well in one now." His brother got to his feet.

He forced himself to stay levelheaded about this and not engage. But Dempsey looked twitchy and judgmental, a combination that didn't sit real well with him right now.

"I need more time to convince her of that." His gaze moved to the second-floor veranda, where her bedroom doors opened onto a private patio. There'd been no movement outside yet, but he'd spoken to the nanny before he left the house and showed her around the place so she knew where to find anything she needed.

"Do I need to remind you why it's important that you do?" Dempsey's voice lowered, but it didn't soften. He'd adopted his steely coaching persona, so it was a face Jean-Pierre recognized from the field.

"Hell no." He understood Dempsey's take on this would be different. The guy had grown up not knowing his father or half brothers. "I'm not Dad. I would never ignore my obligation to my son."

"Then why is Gervais beating you to the altar next weekend?"

"What part of 'I just found out two days ago' did you not understand?" Frustration simmered at the implication he hadn't done enough.

"The part that had my college-educated brother failing to make use of the local justice of the peace." Dempsey made a show of checking his watch. "The clerk's office is open right now."

"It's Saturday." Jean-Pierre had a good plan for using the boat ride to provide a photo opportunity for any media looking for a story. The watercraft rocked gently beneath his feet.

"And lucky for you, I happen to know they have Saturday hours. One of my star players got his girlfriend pregnant last year and I looked it up when I gave my guy the same talk I'm giving you now."

Jean-Pierre shook his head. He normally appreciated Dempsey's down-to-earth take on things, but he couldn't see a way to twist Tatiana's arm to get married. He respected her too much to push her hard when she had been through so much on her own in the last weeks. She'd even admitted she was at an emotionally vulnerable place right now. What kind of man would he be to try and capitalize on that?

"You can spare me the rest of the talk since I already popped the question. The bride said no, for the record. Until I can close that particular deal, I would appreciate some help from the family to show her how welcoming the Reynauds can be."

"You know you don't have to ask. But it's only a matter of time before someone from the press spots her with the baby and then what? The media spotlight you're in now is going to be nothing compared to the juicy news that a player knocked up the coach's daughter."

Jean-Pierre's head snapped up.

"That's my future wife you're talking about."

"That's the spirit." Dempsey clapped him on the shoulder. "The sooner you make it so, the better." He climbed out of the boat and up onto the dock. "One more thing. I forgot the whole reason I came over here."

"What's up?" Jean-Pierre shoved the remaining tools in the tool kit and tucked it into a storage bin on the port side.

"Gervais and Erika are concerned about a media circus if they hold the wedding here as planned. They're going to assemble guests here and then fly them to the private island off Galveston."

The Texas branch of the family was deeply involved in the shipping and cruise business. The island off Galveston was a self-sustaining working ranch and an optional stop on many of their cruise itineraries. Guests could ride horseback on the gulf beaches or take part in one of the farm-to-table feasts that made use of the organically grown vegetables. Jean-Pierre hadn't visited his Texas cousins in years due to a family rift. His grandfather Leon had publicly cut his oldest son, Christophe, out of his will long ago, but since Uncle Christophe still retained his title as a vice president of global operations, he was very much a part of the family business along with his oldest son, Colton.

"Is Kimberly still running the ranch on the island?" She was the youngest of Uncle Christophe's large family, a sweet-natured girl Jean-Pierre remembered fondly from visits to the ranch when they were kids.

"Yes. But Gervais called Colton directly to make sure the island would be available that day. Apparently they're bumping a scheduled cruise from the stop to ensure Gervais and Princess Erika will have total privacy."

"Thanks for the heads-up. I'll let Tatiana know we'll be on the move." He'd been concerned about the extra press attention the wedding would bring to the family. "The additional security will make things easier for her."

Dempsey hesitated.

"What is it?" Jean-Pierre saw movement up by the house and spotted Tatiana on the patio.

He lifted a hand to wave to her.

"Have you read today's headlines about the two of you?" Dempsey reached into his pocket and pulled out a phone.

"I checked in yesterday long enough to assure myself the story about her coming down here with me read roughly as expected." He'd seen her misquoted in a few places, but for the most part, the story ran as Coach's Daughter Bets Against Home Team, or some variation of the basic theme.

Just what he'd anticipated and not the end of the world given the way he'd downplayed it.

"Today they're rehashing that whole court case she won against your friend Marcus Caruthers." Dempsey flipped his phone around to show him the story, complete with sketches from the courtroom showing Tatiana interviewing Marcus on the stand.

The case—which Jean-Pierre considered to be completely unfounded—against one of the game's best running backs had put Marcus out of a contract. Jean-Pierre had done his best to support his friend despite the torrent of bad press he'd received after inflammatory claims of sexual harassment, but the judgment Tatiana had won against him effectively ended his career. The article included quotes Jean-Pierre had given the media at the time, quotes that were now used to suggest a feud between him and Tatiana—one that started with the old family rift and ended with the court battle.

"Marcus didn't deserve this." He thrust the phone back at his brother. "Not then and not now."

"Her client lied. No doubt. But that's not her fault." Dempsey jammed the device back in the pocket of his cargo shorts. "But you must have reached the same conclusion or else you wouldn't be sharing the parenting duties now." He flashed a grin as he backed up a step. "Don't forget about that clerk's office. It's open for four more hours today."

Jean-Pierre gave him a thumbs-up, the most he could manage with the new weight crushing his chest. The truth was, he hadn't come close to making peace with Tatiana for raining hell on his friend's career and personal life. She'd done her job with ruthless precision, winning a judgment for a woman who'd perjured herself, although Tatiana hadn't seen it that way.

He'd been trying not to think about that case in his rush to wrap his head around becoming a father. But maybe today they needed to address the issue that had pushed them both to the boiling point last winter. He'd walked away from her after an unforgettable night—that's how upset he'd been. He'd told her he wouldn't ever make the same mistake, words that had obviously wounded her deeply since she hadn't come to him about her pregnancy sooner.

As he watched her stride down the dock in a fluttery crimson-colored bathing-suit cover-up, he wondered if she'd forgiven him for the things he'd said. It hardly seemed possible since he wasn't sure he'd forgiven her, either. Hopeful mood sinking, he stepped up onto the dock to greet her. He'd face the situation the way he faced any football matchup—grind it out until he got the outcome he sought.

Lucky for him, a victory with this vibrant, sensual woman promised far more satisfying rewards.

Five

To the woman Tatiana had been before her pregnancy, making her way down the dock in a bathing suit just five and a half weeks after giving birth would have been out of the question. But as much as she wished she fit into the sleek black one-piece a bit more easily, she also couldn't deny a certain relief that she had higher priorities now than how good she looked in swimwear. Her body had given her César. And since she loved to swim, she'd made a special appointment with her midwife after she returned to New York to make sure she was safe to go in the water. The laps in her building's heated pool had relaxed her.

If she was a little worse for wear in a bathing suit, so what? She'd figure out what to do with the extra curves next time she went shopping.

Until then thank goodness for cover-ups. The gauzy crimson-paisley tunic felt breezy and pretty as she strode down the wooden planks toward the boat. Right now, she intended to make the most of this break while her son napped under the watchful eye of the nanny.

She could see one of Jean-Pierre's brothers just stepping off the watercraft and she braced herself as he headed toward her.

There was a look to the Reynaud men, making it tricky to tell who was who from a distance. They were all tall with athletic builds. Television didn't do professional athletes justice; because they were viewed in context and next to one another, they all looked a similar size. But when a football player stood next to a regular person, it was impossible not to appreciate the way they were built on a whole different scale.

As the man drew closer, she recognized Dempsey, Jean-Pierre's half brother, from his square jaw and the cleft in his chin, traits he must have inherited from his mother. But his dark hair and brown eyes with hints of green were straight-up Reynaud features.

"Hello, Dempsey." She greeted him with a smile despite the nervous butterflies in her stomach.

How would this family view her after the way she'd kept Jean-Pierre in the dark about his son? In particular, how would this man view her, given he'd been kept from his father as a child?

"Tatiana." He opened his arms and surprised her with a quick embrace. "I'm so glad you're here. I know my brother is anxious to spend time alone with you, but I hope you'll have dinner with the family tonight." A half grin lifted his lips. "That is, if you're up for a reunion with all of us at once. Gervais has a hell of a chef working for him, so we could meet at his place. His fiancée, Erika, wants to see us all so she can share some new details about their wedding."

Tatiana's stomach clenched. A meal with all the Reynauds at once? Nothing like trial by fire. Still, she was heartened by Dempsey's warm reception. The sun seemed to shine a little brighter, glistening off the lightly rolling waves lapping the dock moorings.

"Thank you. That sounds great." She was genuinely curious to meet the women who'd captured the hearts of Jean-Pierre's brothers. The press had plenty to say about each of the three women, but the press wasn't known for being honest. "We'll be there as long as your brother delivers us back here in one piece before dinnertime. I seem to remember he drives a boat like he's eluding the Coast Guard."

Dempsey threw his head back and laughed.

"Some things never change. But I've never seen him lose a passenger yet. I'll let Gervais and Erika know to expect two more." He paused. "Or might that be three?"

Her knees wobbled as a bout of light-headedness shook her. "He told you?"

If so, who else knew? She understood the news needed to be relayed to his family as soon as possible. And truly, she didn't feel any need to be at Jean-Pierre's side when he told them. It had been difficult enough confronting her parents and feeling the weight of their expectations on her shoulders. But even now, she didn't feel emotionally prepared for the fallout this baby would bring.

"He did. And I couldn't be happier for you both. I know the rest of the family will feel the same way." He said it with a steely conviction that suggested he was determined to make it so.

Perhaps he would make a good ally for her son, who'd also been born without the legal protection of her marriage to his father.

"I'm not sure I should come to the big dinner just yet after all because—"

"Whatever you think is best. But don't forget we're

his family. We protect our own." Dempsey lifted a hand to give her shoulder a light squeeze before he set off at a brisk pace down the dock.

Leaving her alone and shaken. The Reynauds protected their own. She believed that. But she couldn't miss the way the words sounded like a proprietary claim. Like the Reynauds had a stake in her son and wouldn't forget it. The resources of this family were beyond imagining. She could never afford a power struggle with such a wealthy, well-connected clan.

Hearing her name called from the water shook her from her thoughts, giving her a welcome distraction from her fears. She looked up to see Jean-Pierre standing on the bow of his yacht peering her way. She didn't need to see his expression to recognize the curiosity and concern in his body language. And didn't that remind her how well she knew him even if they hadn't done more than exchange social niceties for years? Well, except a year ago when they'd exchanged a little more than niceties.

She hurried toward him, telling herself not to be rattled. Not to fall into the trap of thinking she needed his strong arms around her to steady her. Too bad for her, she'd dreamed about sinking into his arms all night long. That and a whole lot more.

"Everything okay?" He straddled the dock and the boat to help her aboard, his sure hand gripping her forearm.

For a moment, their bodies brushed against each other enticingly. The warmth of his thigh tantalized her, evoking a memory of being naked with him while he lay above her...

"Fine," she blurted, leaping back from the contact so fast she had to catch herself against the captain's chair. "Just fine."

His eyes searched hers.

"I hope my brother didn't upset you." He took her by the shoulders and steadied her, his fingers stirring more of the sensual memories she'd tried hard to forget these last months. "We agreed to tell our families about César before we figure out how to go to the press."

"Of course. I'm not upset." She had to keep herself in check or he would see the hunger she was feeling.

His hands stilled on her arms and he studied her for so long she wondered if he recognized what she was feeling. Was her reaction to him more obvious than she realized?

"Don't forget why we planned this outing." His words were softly spoken, a gentle rumble between them while they stood so close.

"To show any press lurking nearby that we're spending time together. That there is no bad blood between us." Although that had honestly been the last thing on her mind after the conversation with Dempsey. Not to mention the upsetting phone call from her father before she'd even rolled out of bed this morning.

A call in which he'd upbraided her for keeping him in the dark about his grandson. Browbeat her for information about when she was going to return to her practice as a trial lawyer instead of the research work she'd taken on recently. Appearances mattered to Jack Doucet and apparently a behind-the-scenes job wasn't good enough for his daughter.

"We are going to have to do better than just demonstrate a lack of enmity. We need to show we're more than just friends, Tatiana. We're building a story so we can introduce César to the world." He lowered his head closer to hers, his lips brushing her hair as he spoke into her ear. "But if you leap away every time I touch you, no one is going to buy it."

The warmth of his body next to hers awakened every

nerve ending. He smelled good, like spices and fresh air. She closed her eyes for just a moment, breathing him in. She lifted her palms to his chest, touching him on instinct. And while she might tell herself that touch maintained a few inches of space between them, she knew better. Having her hands on him was a simple pleasure too good to deny herself after the tumultuous last weeks.

"Agreed." Standing there with him on the lightly rocking deck, she understood the value of what he was suggesting. Pretending a romance between them would only benefit their son.

"Seriously?" He tipped up her chin and the warm sun bathed her cheeks.

"Yes. Your plan makes sense." As worried as she'd been about the reactions of their families to the baby news, she was even more concerned about the way it would play in the press. She'd worked too hard cultivating her career and her professional reputation to be portrayed as a superstar athlete's baby mama.

His dark gaze searched hers. "I'm not used to wrangling an agreement out of the hard-nosed attorney so easily."

"Maybe motherhood has softened my edge." She fought the urge to turn her cheek more firmly into his touch. "It's probably just as well I left litigation behind to focus on legal research."

Releasing her, he frowned. "You're sharp and talented no matter what aspect of the law you're practicing."

She missed his touch even as she felt grateful for the reprieve from the sensual attraction. She watched him untie a cleat hitch on the stern and climb over the bow to follow his lead on the other cleat.

"Thank you." She wasn't accustomed to praise for her work from the people in her life. Usually, her colleagues were a better source of encouragement than her parents.

And, of all people, Jean-Pierre had reason to resent her skills as a lawyer. He'd made it abundantly clear he didn't agree with her efforts to win a judgment against his friend Marcus.

But as they set off onto the lake for the day, she tried to put that behind her to focus on the future. It all started with a believable story, just as he'd said.

She hoped it didn't matter that the romance they were building was strictly for show.

An hour into their boating expedition, Jean-Pierre found the cove he'd been looking for.

He didn't know if Tatiana would even recognize it after so many years, but he was pulling out all the stops to remind her of their past together—a time when they'd been happy. He wasn't ready to talk about her case against Marcus or the way the media was quickly resurrecting that story. He hoped she didn't know about that.

She certainly hadn't mentioned anything about seeing the day's headlines. Instead, they'd focused on having a fun outing with the grim determination of two high achievers. Tatiana had always succeeded at anything she tried thanks to a need to please the people around her—namely her father. As for Jean-Pierre, he'd usually met his goals by refusing to accept any outcome but the one he chose. So they'd both adopted their game faces, mindful of the fact that they were probably being followed by the telephoto lenses of enterprising journalists along the shore.

None of it sat well with him. He craved one real moment with her. Some kind of honest interaction not dictated by what they wanted the cameras to see.

"I can't believe you brought me here." She peered over her shoulder at him from where she lay sunbathing on a deck lounger. She'd slathered on sunscreen, willfully ignoring his repeated offers to help apply it to her back.

The need to touch her grew with every second he spent in her company, but he was trying to play his hand carefully, biding his time until she couldn't resist the current between them any more than he could.

"You remember it?" He pressed the button to lower the anchor on the thirty-six-foot sport yacht.

She shifted positions on the bright yellow towel draped over the lounger.

"We went skinny-dipping here." She arched a dark eyebrow at him.

He noticed how her glossy brown curls had escaped the knot she'd twisted at the back of her head. Everything about her was lusher than he remembered. Her hair had gotten longer and thicker, the curls even more riotous than they'd been ten months ago. And her curves…

He couldn't even think about the eye-popping differences in her figure without facing the uncomfortable physical consequences. He should have noticed right away when he'd seen her at the Coliseum, but she'd been wearing some kind of loose dress that had hidden everything but her mile-long legs. Today, however, in a sleek black one-piece bathing suit, her hourglass shape was the kind that screen sirens had made famous in another era. Extravagant breasts. Generous hips.

He needed to remember she was still recovering from childbirth. But his brain wasn't working on all cylinders right now.

"Did we?" He didn't dare step out from behind the bridge until he had himself under control from just thinking about her, his body's reaction impossible to hide. "It was too dark for me to get a good look that night, so I was never sure if you really took it all off."

"You know perfectly well you copped a feel underwater," she retorted. "Don't pretend."

"I told you that was a fish." He thumped a hand to his chest in mock indignation. "I completely respected your 'no touching' boundaries." He grinned at the memory.

"You had a squirrely brand of ethics even then, Mr. Reynaud." She propped big sunglasses on top of her head and rose to stand at the starboard rail. "It seems funny that mystery fish chose to brush against my left breast."

"If it had been me, I wouldn't have settled for just one." He tried not to think about his odds of touching her this afternoon, although the area around the cove was still secluded, making it a perfect stop for privacy. This section of the lakeshore was no more populated now than it had been ten years ago. Would they get a chance to replay the memory?

"That may be the most convincing argument you've made yet relating to that old disagreement." She turned from the rail to watch him, the sun burnishing her hair in a way that showed subtle streaks of copper. "But since you probably didn't bring me here to skinny-dip, I can't help but wonder what we're doing in this spot."

"We're in the public eye often enough. I thought you'd appreciate some private time." He pointed to her bathing suit. "You seem dressed for a swim even though no native would dream of getting in the water this time of year."

He'd used the fish-finder system to double-check the water nearby and knew there were no rocks or obstacles in the lake. It was deep enough to jump and safe to swim.

"I've been doing laps in gym pools for two weeks with the doctor's okay. And after spending years in New York, this feels like summer weather to me." She tipped her head up to the sun. "And don't try to tell me you wouldn't go in the water. I've seen you jump overboard in January."

"I'll always wade a little if the fish are biting." Focused so narrowly on football, he hadn't been fly-fishing in years. But he'd liked it as a kid, finding comfort in the quietness of the ritual when the rest of his life was so frenetic.

"Was I the only one who thought there might be a swim involved today?" She scraped back some of the loose strands of her hair and tucked them into the knot at the back of her head.

"The air temperature hasn't hit eighty in weeks so there's no telling how cold the water is." He made a show of peering overboard and shivering.

"Guess you're not as warm-blooded as me." She marched the length of the boat toward the swim platform at the back.

He was actually heating up just fine watching her in action, but he kept that to himself.

"Probably not, but I don't think it would be right to let you go all alone." He stalked toward her as she tossed aside her sunglasses. "My camp counselors taught me to use the buddy system when swimming."

She shook her head, a smile curving her lips right before she jumped in with a splash.

And a yelp.

She shrieked about how cold it was, but given how fired up she made him, that could only be a good thing as far as he was concerned. Stripping off his shirt and sliding out of his shoes, he stepped down to the platform to see for himself.

He aimed his jump to land a few feet from Tatiana. She swam with sure strokes through the dark water, her skin pale beneath the surface. He caught her around the ankle for a moment, relishing the feel of her silky soft skin. Allowing her to wriggle free, he treaded water and watched her cavort around in the waves.

"I thought it was too cold for you." She paused when she saw he'd stopped moving. Her long dark lashes had turned into spiky fringes around her bottle green eyes.

"I was afraid there might be more fish out to get you." He hadn't been kidding about the buddy system.

Not to mention, this was the mother of his child. He had every reason to protect her.

"I think I felt one around my ankle a minute ago." She seemed more relaxed out here.

"Did you ever miss it here?" He swam closer, drawn to her when she smiled and teased like the woman he'd once known.

Her smile faded.

"If I did, I wasn't allowed to show it." She shrugged, sending ripples out through the water near her. "I learned to love New York."

And she'd left him in the dust the same way she'd ditched the Big Easy.

"Remember that time I went to visit you during spring break after you moved to New York and you wouldn't see me?" He'd defied his older brothers and caught a commercial flight to Manhattan. Pounded on her family's door until her father threatened to call the cops.

"Of course. You said you wouldn't leave until you saw me." She held herself very still. "My father eventually made me come out of my room to tell you to go home."

"I understood that you were seventeen and had to do what they said. I didn't expect you to jump into a cab with me and run away to Spain or something." Even though he'd proposed just that at one point. But that was mostly because one of her father's favorite players was harassing her and Jack let the guy get away with it. "I just hoped you'd use the chance to tell your dad he didn't always know what was best for you."

Jean-Pierre had been angry at the time that she'd knuckled under so easily. But he hadn't understood how important it was to her to be accepted. To earn her father's approval. Maybe he still didn't get it.

Then again, his parents had never expected much from him or any of their sons. His dad had been a player all his life, and not just on the football field. Hence their half brother Dempsey, who was so close in age to Gervais it had been the last straw for his mother. She'd left the family shortly after Theo had moved Dempsey into their home.

Jean-Pierre had worked too damn hard to differentiate himself from his father to ever be viewed as some kind of womanizer.

"I learned to decide what was best for me eventually." She swam by him toward the boat. "At least, I hope I did."

Water sluiced off her as she hauled herself up the ladder and into the boat. Not finished with this conversation, Jean-Pierre followed her. He'd waited too long to talk to her after that time she'd told him she didn't ever want to see him again. And then, ten years later when he'd been so angry about the court case that he confronted her, the feelings had been so strong and so convoluted he didn't know what they'd acted on that night. Passion? Resentment? Anger? A toxic mix of all three?

And yet...not toxic. She'd conceived that night, and he wanted to understand what had happened between them so they could provide a healthy environment for a child in the future.

"I forgot a towel," she called over her shoulder. "Do you have extras?"

"I do." He pulled one out of the warming drawer beneath a bench seat. "But do you want to sit in the front deck hot tub for a few minutes to warm up?"

He tossed her the towel and toed aside the leather cover

of the small tub built into the bow. Steam wafted up, surrounding them both in a soft white mist.

Her eyes went wide as she snuggled deeper into the towel. "I can't believe there was a hot tub under there." She came closer to see for herself. "I thought that covered up a holding tank for fish or something."

"Hardly." He folded the leather cover in half and pulled it the rest of the way off. "I'm not eighteen anymore, Tatiana. I allow myself a few creature comforts these days."

She bit her lip and unfastened the hair tie that had held her curls. "I don't want to stay out too much longer. I need to feed César soon."

Still, he would bet money she was tempted. And seeing her shift her weight uncertainly from one long, sleek leg to the other had him feeling damn tempted, too.

"I can get us back home in about half the time I took to travel out here. How about we get in the tub just long enough to warm up?" He went with the reasonable approach. But then, remembering what she'd said about runaway emotions since giving birth, he tried another appeal. "Besides, you've been so focused on caring for César that it doesn't seem like you've made much time to relax and recover. You won't be much good to him if you wear yourself out."

Her gaze flipped up to meet his for a moment before she dipped her toes in the steaming pool. He reached over to the side of a deck box and switched on the air jets. The motor hummed as bubbles erupted on the surface of the water, sending even more steam into the air.

"Maybe for a few minutes," she agreed, slipping out of the towel and stepping down into the hot tub.

He shifted closer to steady her arm, following her into the swirl of frothy water.

The purr of contentment she made as she settled into a

seat beside him stirred him as quickly as a physical touch, the sound reverberating down his spine to remind him how much he wanted her. How much he wanted to inspire that same moan of satisfaction from her.

"Feel good?" Being around her had always revved him high and this day with her was testing his every last restraint.

He allowed his gaze to roam over her the way his hands wanted to, which was easier to do with her eyes closed and her head tipped back against a neck pillow. Her loosened hair floated around her shoulders. She was like a mermaid dragging him down to his doom. High, full breasts showed above the surface, in easy reach of his mouth. And at this rate, he felt as if the temperature in the hot tub had been cranked a few degrees higher.

"Feels amazing." She still didn't open her eyes. "My body has been through the wringer these last weeks. And not just from childbirth. Even carrying him around…that sounds silly, I know." She straightened and glanced over at him. "He's only nine pounds. But still, I'm not used to the position and I get all kinked up."

She rolled her shoulders and then her neck.

He tightened his self-restraint, until it felt like an iron vise.

"Turn around." He caught one shoulder in his hand and guided her so that her back was to him. "I'm good at this."

"That's really not necessary," she protested, but when he got both hands on those trapezius muscles, all objections ceased. "Ooh."

She melted beneath his touch. And while he would have liked it to be even more intimate, it satisfied the hell out of him that he could give her this pleasure.

"Relax," he urged her, shifting their positions so she sat between his legs. "This is going to help."

He felt her tense for a moment as her hip grazed the inside of his thigh beneath the water. But then, as he worked his fingertips deeper into the deltoid muscles, she went limp again, her head lolling forward while he massaged her back and neck.

The bubbles rushed toward her skin and burst in an endless cycle of movement from the jets.

"I had no idea you possessed this skill." Her voice hummed through his fingertips, the sound a vibration he could feel as he worked a kink from her left side. "I've paid big bucks for professional massages that haven't felt this good."

"Working with trainers really increased my awareness of the muscle groups. I wouldn't have maintained a career for this long without good sports therapy." He tried to focus on the conversation and not how good she felt. How soft and supple beneath his hands.

And how good she smelled.

Even after the swim in the lake followed by the chlorinated spa tub, a fragrant hint of lemons clung to her skin and hair. He breathed deep, inhaling her scent as he molded her body with his touch.

"You get a lot of massages?" She tilted her head from side to side slowly before she turned to peer back at him.

"Yes, but not many of the kind that feel good. I tend to get the deep-tissue stuff that leaves bruises."

"Ouch." She winced in sympathy. "I'm sure I wouldn't like that."

"I don't always like it, either, but it can really help alleviate muscle strains."

"Like your triceps last season?"

"Exactly. I injured my arm when I hyperextended—hey. How did you know about that?" He paused, looking over her shoulder to see her face.

The movement of the boat in the waves sloshed a little water out of the tub to spill on the deck.

"I might have been paying attention to some of your games." She spun around to face him, her hair fanning out in the water as she whirled. "That felt great by the way. Thank you."

"I like touching you," he said simply, surprised that she'd followed his career. "I always have."

One dark curl clung damply to her neck, snagging his eye. He slid a finger beneath it, barely brushing her skin, intending to relocate the strands behind her back. But that was before he felt the leap of her pulse in her throat. A quick, erratic rhythm that he could almost see in the tender column of her neck.

He didn't want to press her. But his hand didn't seem to be taking instruction from his brain. He laid his palm against her damp skin to get a better feel of that thready, anxious beat. Her eyes closed on contact, her head tipping back in a way that brought her lips within kissing range.

Sensual hunger washed over him like a rogue wave. He slid his fingers around the base of her neck and steered her mouth to his. Warning bells blared in his head that he couldn't let things get out of control like last time. He knew that. So with every bit of willpower he possessed, he kissed her gently. Softly, but with a lingering lick along her lower lip. And a nip at the end because she had the most lush, inviting lips he'd ever tasted.

But then, he let her go. Even though it cost him dearly, he untangled his hand from her hair and released her. Sitting back in the tub with wide eyes, her lips parted slightly, she looked as surprised as he felt.

There would be time enough for more, when she was ready. For now, he had to let her come to him so that whatever happened next was her choice. It was a good plan.

Smart. Logical. And it didn't do a damn thing to ease a body on fire for her. Taking deep breaths as he willed his urges into submission, he knew he wouldn't be climbing out of that hot tub anytime soon.

Six

"I can't believe you convinced me to bring César to this dinner party." Flustered in every way possible, Tatiana navigated the whitewashed stone walkway in kitten heels, holding tight to Jean-Pierre's arm out of stress more than a need for balance.

They strode side by side up a pathway from his home to his brother's residence, a huge mansion on the hill that she'd visited many times as a teen. First with her father, when he'd spend time with Leon Reynaud during the spring months to plan for their team, and later on her own when she'd dated Jean-Pierre for those brief months in prep school.

Now, Gervais, the owner of the New Orleans Hurricanes and Jean-Pierre's oldest brother, made the big house his own along with his soon-to-be wife, Princess Erika Mitras. No doubt the home would be different than Tatiana remembered. Normally, she would look forward to a visit like this, but tonight there was so much stress riding on her shoulders she couldn't work up the energy to be excited to meet royalty. Jean-Pierre was getting under her skin, for one thing. Her whole body still hummed from their too brief encounter on his boat, her every nerve ending now sensually attuned to his touch. But worse than that, she was starting to feel more than just attracted to him. His care and concern over her well-being made her question what she knew about him. Made her rethink all the reasons she was fighting her attraction.

And on top of everything else, he wanted to bring their newborn with them tonight. Not the reveal she had in mind.

"It's funny you think that, because I don't see you holding César." Jean-Pierre wrapped his arm around her waist to steady her and she couldn't think of a single good reason to pull away.

The kiss on the boat had shifted something between them, forcing her to admit they had a whole lot of unfinished business.

"I know." Her heart beat faster, her nerves twitching as they neared the huge Greek revival mansion. Out front, a black Range Rover was parked grille-to-grille across from a Ferrari. "But Lucinda will be bringing him shortly. And it seems like a lot to bombard your brothers with at once—telling them you have a son and then actually having them meet a baby."

"Not just any baby." His voice held a note of unmistakable pride. "Our son. And the first thing my brothers will ask once we tell them about César is when they can meet him. Trust me. They would feel slighted if we didn't introduce them to their nephew."

She peered up at him in the gray, single-breasted suit that he wore exceedingly well. The white dress shirt, open at the neck and worn with no tie, was his nod to a more casual gathering, but the man looked good enough to touch, to eat. She could see the lines of the comb through his hair, still damp from the shower he'd taken when they returned from the boat, and her fingers ached to smooth over them.

"I'll let you take the conversational lead then." She had enough worries just thinking about how to address a princess and how to assure the rest of the Reynaud brothers that she didn't hold a grudge against them the way her father did.

"Of course." He squeezed her gently, his grip tightening around her waist and drawing her closer. "And don't be so tense or I'll have no choice but to give you more massages."

A tingle of pleasure went through her, her whole body warming with a sensual promise she shouldn't be feeling. Then again, she wasn't even cleared for intimacy from her doctor, so it wasn't as though anything would happen. Maybe she shouldn't be fighting this so hard—the massage, the kisses, all of which she couldn't deny wanting.

"That might not be such a bad thing," she admitted softly as they climbed the steps toward the front entrance, camellias in bloom in urns near the entrance.

"I want to take care of you." With just two fingers, he stroked her hip, a small gesture with an incredible impact she felt through the thin layers of her jade-colored dress. "In whatever way you'll let me."

Her mind went in all kinds of seductive directions. He'd taken care of her with exquisite care in their explosive night together. For that matter, back when they were dating, she'd been a virgin, but even then Jean-Pierre had taught her memorable lessons about other ways to find satisfaction. He'd taken good care of her then, too, even if they'd refrained from ever having sex.

Until the night they'd made César. They had been long

past virginity days, but they'd still had a first time together. Their only time?

Tongue-tied, she smoothed back her loose hair and tried to recover.

"You're blushing," he said in her ear, the soft whisper almost a caress in itself. "And it's killing me."

She braved a look at him then, only to find he was watching her with the same hunger she was feeling. If they hadn't been headed to a family dinner party, she might have dragged him back to his house. But just then, he pressed the doorbell.

"Welcome home, Mr. Reynaud." An attractive gray-haired woman in a pressed black uniform stood aside to let them enter. "Won't you come in?"

Tatiana's stomach muscles clenched as they stepped into the echoing foyer. She took in the white marble floors and walls covered in hand-painted murals depicting a fox hunt. An impressive banister wrapped around a huge staircase with a landing that looked big enough for a cocktail party.

"They're outside," the servant informed them, gesturing for them to go through a room on the left. "We're serving cocktails by the fire."

The woman hurried ahead to open a second set of doors, but Jean-Pierre shook his head.

"I know the way. Thank you." After dismissing the help, he returned his attention to Tatiana as they walked through an opulent dining room surrounded by silk curtains and set aglow by the light of a breathtaking chandelier. Fresh flowers dotted the table at regular intervals.

Nerves tightening with every step, she smoothed a hand over her hair. She'd left it loose after her shower, but now she wished she'd gone with a more polished style.

"You look beautiful." Jean-Pierre's voice startled her, mostly because he seemed to have read her mind.

No. He guessed she was nervous because she was fidgeting with her hair like a preteen. She should have worn one of her navy court suits that gave her the mental armor for battle, clothes that reminded her she was smart and well prepared for her job.

"Thank you." She appreciated his thoughtfulness even as she resented him for seeing that vulnerability. She needed to work out a plan for co-parenting with him, not rely on him for muscle massages and emotional support. This was the same man who'd walked out on her after the most passionate encounter of her life. "I'll be fine. I'm ready."

Nodding, he seemed to accept her at her word. He led her out of the dining room and into a more casual family space with an entertainment bar and Palladian windows overlooking the pool and grounds. A slow Cajun love song drifted on the breeze, the accordion and fiddle pouring out a heartfelt zydeco tune. Torches were lit at regular intervals around the pool in addition to landscape lighting that highlighted ornamental plantings and statues. To one side of the pool, she thought she spied an outdoor kitchen. But the hearth area was unmistakable, a fire already ablaze in the stone surround. Built-in stone seating was covered with thick cushions protected by a pergola, where another wrought-iron chandelier hung, this one more casual.

She couldn't see the faces of the people out there, but she heard their laughter, saw the movement of a couple slow-dancing to one side of the pool.

"They don't bite," Jean-Pierre promised, waiting for her while she took it all in.

"You forget I met Henri before he was fully domesticated." She had always liked the Reynaud brothers. When they were younger, she loved to see them wrestle and play, always in competition with each other, from sports to board games to who could eat their cereal faster.

Sometimes, when her father would spend a week with Leon to plot and plan a strategy for trades, she would roam free with the boys on their big ranch in Texas, or else they'd stay here. The best part of the Louisiana house had always been the lake. Before they were old enough to take out boats, they'd still built sand castles or tried to dam a little waterway that ran into Pontchartrain. She hadn't needed to worry about appearances with them back when Jack Doucet had viewed Leon Reynaud as a trusted friend. It was only afterward that her father had warned her never to reveal the financial hardship brought on by the rift. That part was in the past, but the resentment hadn't faded.

"He channels the fierce side into game days now." He paused at the screen door leading out onto the patio. "Although you'd never know he had a fierce side lately to look at him with Fiona." He pointed to the couple she'd seen dancing by the pool.

The two moved as one, the woman's long black skirt wrapping around the man's thigh when he turned her, their steps synched to a private beat. Just looking at them made Tatiana's heart ache. There'd been a time she'd longed for that kind of romance in her life. Now, her heart was full of love for César and she was glad for it. But a mother's all-consuming tenderness for her child was a far cry from the emotional bond so obviously shared by the dancers.

Everyone on the pool patio looked happy, in fact. The two couples seated near the fireplace spoke animatedly. An extravagant blonde held court with a story that required both hands to tell. Tatiana almost hated to interrupt them. It would have been awkward enough setting foot in the Reynaud home after the way Leon had fired her father. And her dad had reciprocated, bashing the family's lauded football savvy in the press, calling Leon a mircro-managing control freak who couldn't share the spotlight with anyone who knew more than him. The quotes came to mind easily even now. But that wasn't all; tonight she had to get reacquainted with the family at the same time she introduced them to them to the child she'd kept secret.

"Here we go." Jean-Pierre palmed the small of her back, guiding her through the door out into the night air.

The scent of burning firewood wafted on the breeze, mingling with the chlorine tinge of the pool. Six sets of eyes turned toward them as they strode closer.

"It's the prodigal son returned," Jean-Pierre called to them. "I'm back on the bayou and ready for a wedding."

Tatiana couldn't process who shouted what, but he was greeted with a chorus of male taunts with every step.

"I hope you can find a tie before the wedding."

"I thought I was the prodigal son?"

"Technically, we're not on the bayou, dude."

But despite the ribbing, his brothers descended on him, giving him a variety of punches, backslaps and complicated handshakes that looked more fit for the gridiron than cocktail hour. They were an absurdly good-looking family with their tall, athletic builds, dark hair and dark eyes. Their mother had passed along their coloring while their father had donated his size and strength. Would César look like them as he grew up?

Tatiana was only too glad to fade into the background for the moment, but she could feel the keen eye of her hostess and the other women even before Gervais separated himself from the men.

"Tatiana." His nod was reserved as he extended a hand. He had always been the most refined of the brothers, aware of his role as head of the family even as a teen. Tonight, he was dressed like a man worthy of a princess, his flawless silk suit custom-tailored to fit his wide shoulders. "It's good to see you again."

"Is that any way to greet my biggest fan?" Henri elbowed past Dempsey and Gervais, his slim-cut jacket a smooth fit over a dark T-shirt. He pulled her in for a hug. "Welcome back to Cajun country, darlin', and thank you kindly for single-handedly increasing my odds of winning next week's Hurricanes versus Gladiators matchup, according to the latest Vegas line."

Henri cut a glance at his brother, clearly angling to aggravate Jean-Pierre. Before he could respond, however, Dempsey pulled Henri away and stood beside her, his gray jacket as crisp as the gray linen shirt beneath it. His white-and-gray-striped tie was pinned into place with a silver football tac.

"Don't mind Henri," Dempsey warned. "He's had locker-room manners for so long we don't know if we can fix him."

"You *all* flunk the manners class," the platinum-haired beauty informed them from her seat beside the fire. Only now was it evident the woman was pregnant, the empire waist of her dress settling on a baby bump. "Some of us have not been introduced to our guest."

Jean-Pierre escorted Tatiana over to Gervais's fiancée, who must not have been quite as frightening as she sounded since none of the Reynauds appeared chastened in the least.

"Erika, my apologies. Thank you for having us. Please meet Tatiana Doucet." His hand was steady on her spine, a warmth that gave her courage.

Because no matter how the family responded to her now, they were bound to behave differently once they found out about the son she'd kept a secret from Jean-Pierre. That is, if they didn't know already. Would Dempsey have mentioned it? But looking into the cool blue gaze of her hostess, Tatiana couldn't glean a guess one way or the other. Which was rare for her since she'd always been good at sizing up a jury.

"A pleasure to meet you." Her fingers closed around Tatiana's, a collection of delicate silver rings pressing against her skin. But Tatiana's gaze was all for the impressive sparkler on the woman's left hand; it seemed to throw rainbows of reflected firelight into the dark evening. "We have all been curious who Jean-Pierre would bring to the wedding. You can imagine our surprise when we heard his date announced in a press interview rather than an RSVP."

Henri's wife, Fiona, a woman Tatiana had only seen in photographs online, came to stand beside Erika. A petite brunette with a ponytail almost to her waist flanked the princess's other side.

Tatiana took a moment to formulate a response, but the woman with the ponytail leaped into the momentary silence.

"Actually, Dempsey announced our engagement in a postgame conference, so I wasn't at all surprised." She thrust out her hand. "I'm Adelaide."

"So nice to meet you." Tatiana remembered reading that Dempsey had proposed to his longtime personal assistant, a friend from his childhood.

"I'm Fiona, Henri's wife," the other woman said, shaking Tatiana's hand. "And I'm thrilled to have finally evened out the gender gap at family events, so you are most welcome, Tatiana."

"Thank you. I'm grateful for the chance to reconnect with the Reynauds." Her gaze slid over the faces of each brother as they crowded closer to their respective women. She really had missed their friendship even though she'd never been as close to the others as she'd been to Jean-

Pierre. "I didn't realize until recently what a mistake it's been to allow my father's quarrels to become my own."

"There is a family dispute?" Erika frowned, turning her crystalline-blue gaze to Gervais. "I thought the problem stemmed from the court case—" She must have sensed the sudden tension in the group because she cut herself off midsentence. "Forgive me. I have been away from diplomacy for too long and my skills are rusty."

Tatiana's cheeks heated as the blaze in the fireplace flared high.

"There is nothing to forgive. Long after my father argued with Leon, I added fuel to an old fire by taking a case that pitted me against a well-known football player who is a friend to this family." She hadn't known the connection at the time—not until the case had gone to trial.

She swallowed hard, feeling the convivial atmosphere fading. Even easygoing Henri wouldn't meet her eyes.

"But the case is done," Jean-Pierre reminded her—and everyone else—while a server moved silently around the patio setting up trays and glasses. "And I've never held her father's choices against her. So I thought it was well past time for her to return to New Orleans."

Uncomfortable as she was about subterfuge, she shifted slightly closer to him, grateful for his support among people who respected Marcus Caruthers, the player whose career she'd effectively ended.

No, she reminded herself. The man who had effectively ended his own career by firing an assistant after she'd complained about sexual harassment in the workplace. Tatiana steeled her spine again; she needed to recover her lawyerly disposition even more than she needed her prebaby body.

"Actually, Jean-Pierre is being kind. He came to my rescue after I made a very offhanded remark to a man I didn't realize was a reporter." She'd been a babbling, nervous wreck before she had finally confronted Jean-Pierre about their son. She needed to be careful she didn't become a babbling nervous wreck all over again. Cursing postpartum hormones, she turned to Erika, feeling as if she owed her hostess an explanation. "So I was as surprised as anyone that he invited me to be his guest for the week. It was quick thinking on his part to deflect interest from my comment, and I'm truly grateful he did since I didn't mean it and because it gave me the chance to reconnect with all the Reynauds."

A beat of silence followed. Beside her, she sensed Jean-Pierre's tension in the way he held himself. For her part, however, she felt relieved to share the truth.

The family shared uneasy glances. What had she said?

"We had hoped you were a couple," Adelaide explained, perhaps seeing her confusion. "Photographs from your boat ride today are already appearing online, so we hoped—"

"Let's have a toast," Gervais proposed, coming to Adelaide's rescue. He waved forward a server who'd been setting up a small outdoor bar. "It's time we celebrated your return, no matter how unorthodox the circumstances."

The young man tending the bar brought a tray full of glasses in one hand and two distinctive black bottles of champagne in the other. Another server, a woman dressed in a tuxedo shirt and pants that matched the man's, joined him to help him pop the tops and quickly pour champagne for everyone but Erika, who was given a fresh glass of seltzer. Tatiana decided a small, social sip of champagne would not derail her nursing.

Gervais didn't miss a beat, raising his cut-crystal flute as soon as it was placed in his hand. Everyone else followed suit and waited for his toast. Tatiana could hear the waves of the lake against the shore nearby in the quiet.

"To Jean-Pierre and Tatiana, reunited after too long."

Grateful for the way the eldest Reynaud smoothed over the strained moment, she relaxed for the first time since she'd walked in the front door. But before she could lift her glass to her lips, the maid who'd admitted them reappeared at Jean-Pierre's side.

"Excuse me." She spoke in soft tones that Tatiana could overhear. "I believe the guest you invited is here, sir."

"Of course. Hold that thought, Gervais." Jean-Pierre strode toward the back of the patio, where Lucinda was standing at the door, a small bundle in her arms.

All at once, Tatiana remembered that the biggest hurdle of the night still awaited them.

And while the timing felt a bit awkward to her, Jean-Pierre grinned, as if a big reveal had been his intention all along.

Her knees turned to water as she stood alone with the rest of the family. All eyes turned to Jean-Pierre as he escorted Lucinda into the firelight with her precious charge cradled in her arms.

A collective gasp sounded. Tatiana could feel the shock travel from one Reynaud to the next, like Sunday football fans performing the wave around a crowded stadium.

"When Tatiana said she was glad to reconnect, she didn't mention the reason we are happiest to be together." He stared at her in the shifting shadows from the burning torches all around the party, his expression full of paternal pride.

"Meet our son, César."

Seven

Somehow, the zydeco music continued playing on Gervais Reynaud's expansive patio and pool deck. The servers poured more champagne and Gervais offered a toast to César Reynaud, the first of the next generation. People helped themselves to hors d'oeuvres while conversation slowly recovered.

Tatiana sat on a far ottoman, nibbling on a grits-and-gumbo crostini topped with a tiny shrimp skewer. She knew it was delicious, as it incorporated all the flavors of the famed Cajun stew. But she barely registered the taste.

Everyone offered congratulations. Of course they did.

She'd murmured polite acknowledgments and enough commentary to be social, but as the focus shifted fully to the baby, she was able to clear her head long enough to take a much-needed deep breath and calm down. Because all the while Jean-Pierre showed off his firstborn, she seethed at the way her son's introduction to his family had been tainted by half-truths.

Since the Reynauds had been given no explanation for why Tatiana and Jean-Pierre had kept their baby news quiet, she knew without question his family would blame her for keeping César a secret. Surely they all believed that if Jean-Pierre knew about the baby before now, he would have told them. And, no doubt, he would have.

So even as they passed around the sleeping newborn in his cream-colored footie with a velour shawl collar, they must have guessed that Tatiana had been the one keeping secrets.

But what Jean-Pierre had failed to share with them was her reason for not including him in their son's birth. He had called their union a mistake. He'd walked out on her the morning after their one-night stand, making it clear that he'd only been on board for one night.

What was she supposed to do when that first pregnancy test had come back positive? How could she share such incredible, life-changing news with a man who might view their son as...another mistake? She swallowed hard, reminding herself that her fear had passed. Seeing Jean-Pierre hold César so tenderly now, and hearing the obvious pride in his voice as he talked about their son, it was almost inconceivable that she'd once feared early on that Jean-Pierre might have suggested she terminate her pregnancy.

But with the way they'd parted, she had most certainly feared the worst.

"Excuse me," she said to no one in particular, backing away from the crowd around César. She needed a moment to herself, the ugly thoughts spinning so fast she felt dizzy. "I'll be right back."

Hurrying inside the house, she rushed through the beautifully appointed spaces, passing a server on the way who told her where to find a powder room.

"Tatiana?" She heard Jean-Pierre's voice and quick footsteps behind her, and slowed down before she could reach her destination.

She ducked into a nearby doorway, a den she had noticed vaguely when she'd first arrived tonight. The powder-room visit would wait since she didn't want to have this conversation over the sink. Here, leather club chairs and a small bar flanked a darkened fireplace, while books and football memorabilia lined the walls. A banker's desk lamp glowed softly over a masculine expanse of polished oak.

"Are you all right?" He followed her into the den, taking her hands in both of his. "We don't need to stay for dinner if you don't feel up to it. Everyone will understand you're tired from the travel and still recovering from having a baby."

Had she felt a warm connection to him earlier today on the boat? It was difficult to remember now with her stomach in knots.

"I will not let your family think even worse of me than they already do. I don't want them to assume I'm ignoring them." She allowed him to draw her down to a buttery soft leather settee, but then withdrew her hands from his. "I am staying for dinner."

"No one thinks poorly of you." Tipping his head to one side, he considered her. "And I guarantee everyone out there is sympathetic to the fact that you gave birth less than six weeks ago."

"Are they?" She folded her arms across breasts that felt more functional than attractive lately. She ached to hold her child already. Sharing him with this large, charismatic family was tougher than she'd expected.

Not that she should care about that right now. But this man had always called to her on the most fundamental level; not even her anger with him could diminish that. As they'd discovered last winter.

"Of course they are." Seated beside her, he stared at her as if she'd lost her grip on reality. "In case you haven't noticed, Erika is very pregnant with twins. Gervais can't be there for her enough, doing everything in his power to make her life easier so her strength goes toward nurturing their children. Do you honestly think anyone would begrudge you recovery time after delivering my child?"

"Our. Our child." She did feel exhausted suddenly, but she didn't know if it had to do with postpartum tiredness or the stress of negotiating her role in parenting with this man. "I am not here to hand him over to you, Jean-Pierre, or to your family, so don't get in the habit of claiming him as yours alone."

"Of course. My God, of course I know that. I would never deny our child his mother." Even in the darkened room, his gaze burned with a tangle of emotions she couldn't interpret. "Tatiana, I understand this isn't easy on you, but I thought it best to come straight to the point with my family."

Unlike the way she'd done in telling him about their child? She couldn't help but note how differently they'd shared the news.

"But we both wanted to tell our families and now those closest to us know the truth," he continued. "Next, we can focus on carefully unveiling the story we want to share with the media."

"You know what?" She smoothed nervous hands over the short silk skirt of her dress. The brush of the fabric against her skin was the most sensual touch she'd felt on her legs in months. "I disagree that our families learned the whole truth. All your brothers have found out is that I kept your son a secret from you."

"I never said that." His jaw flexed, the shadows falling across his face in the dim room.

She sprang up from her seat, unwilling to sit so close to him with this restless anger churning in her blood.

"Maybe. But by not saying anything to explain our belated revelation, you allow them to think the worst of me and that starts us out badly when our families already have issues."

"And what would you have me say?" He rose from the settee as well, but he moved in the opposite direction from her. They faced off on either side of the study, backs to the walls of books. "Because I'm fairly unclear on why I got scratched from your contact list while you gave birth to *our* child by yourself."

"Then let me be very clear." Frustration simmered and her patience snapped. "The last words you said to me before I found out I was pregnant was that you would never repeat the mistake of being with me."

"That's not fair."

"You asked. And while it might not feel fair to you, it didn't feel fair to me that you could hold me in contempt for doing my job in the courtroom." She braced her back against the bookshelves, needing the support of something—anything—in her life right now. "After we...had sex that night, I foolishly assumed you realized that you were wrong to find fault with me for winning my case. I woke up happy. Did you even know I was making you breakfast when you stormed out of that room? I had the concierge find me fresh eggs and a pan so I could make them myself in that tiny kitchen."

She hadn't meant to share all that, dammit. It was far too revealing.

For a moment, he didn't speak. When he did, he cursed softly.

"I didn't hold the verdict against you." He pounded his fist gently against the bookshelf closest to him. "I just thought you might want to know what I'd seen as Marcus's friend. His assistant was—is—an untrustworthy woman."

"I can't choose the clients my firm takes on, and I won't argue that with you again." She'd heard as much as she wanted to hear of his side during the case. "When I thought we'd put that behind us, I was all the more hurt to discover you regretted being with me."

"So you didn't tell me about César to punish me?" The gaze he leveled at her made her wonder how they'd ever find common ground to raise their son.

Some of the fight leaked out of her and she raked a hand through her hair.

"I didn't tell you because I couldn't bear to hear that having César was a mistake."

Two hours later, Jean-Pierre walked out of the most uncomfortable meal of his life. Knowing what Tatiana thought of him—that he'd been denied the early weeks of his son's life because she assumed he was the worst sort of human being—had made it damn near impossible to choke down food and pretend everything was all right in his world.

He'd quietly walked back to his home with Tatiana, making sure she was safely inside before he left again. After their exchange in the den, she'd had little to say to him anyhow, and their quick stroll back to his house had been devoid of conversation save an agreement to speak again tomorrow when cooler heads prevailed.

Before then, he needed a plan for how to proceed with her, something he wasn't going to accomplish until he could blow off some steam.

He headed to the three-bay garage on one side of the house and hit the button for the closest door. The reinforced steel retracted silently to reveal the BMW M6 he kept registered in Louisiana. The silver Gran Coupé wasn't as flashy as the Aston Martin he used in Manhattan, but it would get him to the Hurricanes' training complex in a hurry. Slipping into the driver's seat, he nailed the accelerator and left the family compound behind.

Perhaps it was a conflict of interest for him to work out in a competing team's training facility before he faced them. But he wouldn't be anywhere near the players' areas. And hell, he was one of the family.

Twenty minutes later, when he parked in the owner's spot with the assurance that Gervais wouldn't show up for work for at least six more hours, Jean-Pierre took the private elevator to the gym for the front office personnel. He was a Reynaud, dammit. He had a key. He'd invested personally in building the facility, as well as the Zephyr Dome downtown. And he'd never needed a workout as much as he did now.

Helping himself to Dempsey's locker—helpfully labeled with a brass nameplate—he found workout clothes and changed into black mesh shorts and a T-shirt. He ran the track. Ran the bleachers, ran the treadmill. And when that didn't manage to pound the thoughts out of his head, he hit the weights. He dragged a set of heavy chains from the wall and draped them around his waist while he did pull-ups. He did waist-high box jumps from a standing position with an eighty-pound-weight vest. If it hadn't been a bye week, he wouldn't have been able to trash his body so thoroughly, but he had time to recover before the game against the Hurricanes.

And sweating out the sound of Tatiana's damning words had become a critical mission.

I didn't tell you because I couldn't bear to hear that having César was a mistake.

Drenched with sweat and so exhausted he feared the

next jump would sprain an ankle, he unhooked the chains and finally slogged to the showers. Only then did it occur to him what he needed to do to move forward with Tatiana.

She didn't trust him now any more than she had when she first found out she was expecting their child. He had to change that. Luckily, no matter what she said about the effects of postpartum hormones, she was a lawyer and a deeply rational woman. She would appreciate a well-thought-out campaign to win her over. Well-reasoned arguments for why they should stay together.

He would dismantle her defenses as thoroughly as he deconstructed his opponents on the field. While he couldn't study game film of Tatiana, he had past encounters to teach him. He could use that to understand her better. To draw on what she liked and didn't like to become the man she couldn't refuse.

And then? Game over.

He would be announcing their marriage at the same time he introduced César to the media and then they could both put this chapter of their lives behind them. It was the perfect game plan.

Provided he could persuade her to agree.

Eight

Even when angry, Tatiana dreamed about him.

Perversely, that made her even madder, distracting her all morning when she'd had errands to run outside the house. How could she go to bed so upset with Jean-Pierre and yet dream about his touch all night long?

She'd awoken on edge and cranky even though César had slept through the night for the first time ever. She'd almost missed her morning doctor's appointment, a checkup she'd scheduled with a local obstetrician to be sure she was healing. An appointment that had given her clearance for intimacy at a time when she knew that was highly unlikely to happen since Jean-Pierre hadn't even wanted to sleep in the same house as her the night before.

Now, changing into fresh clothes after the morning's outing, she wished she'd had the option to hop in a luxury sports car the night before and disappear the way Jean-Pierre had.

From the patio outside her suite, she'd watched him roar off, the tension evident in his every movement. She hadn't heard him come home, but he'd texted her, asking to join him at Gervais's house today to help with some kind of wedding crisis. She couldn't begin to guess what that meant, but once she'd eaten a light meal and fed and snuggled with César, she put on a crochet knit minidress with bright stripes around the skirt and headed outside to see what was happening. The temperature had dropped overnight so that the air was milder this afternoon, but still comfortable enough that she didn't need a sweater.

Her phone rang before she reached Gervais's house. Checking the display, she spotted her father's cell phone number.

She took a deep breath before she answered. "Hello, Dad," she said as she wound through the manicured gardens of a side yard between the Reynaud homes.

She kept her tone light, praying he would reciprocate. She couldn't handle any more tension right now.

"Are you reading the headlines?" he barked, not bothering to ask her how she'd been.

Which reminded her of why she couldn't bind herself to Jean-Pierre, another man who focused on himself and to hell with her needs. Sure, he'd caught her off guard with his careful treatment of her and the thoughtful massage, but how much of that kindness was to serve his own ends? She needed to be wary.

"I've been fairly consumed with motherhood," she reminded her father, wondering why she'd struggled for so long to win approval from a man who cared more about how his family appeared to the rest of the world than how they felt.

"Well, you've done a good job keeping that under wraps," he admitted. The sounds of the city were amplified in the background—squealing air brakes and honking horns. He must be in the car between meetings. "And the photos of your boat outing are a nice touch, much as it still galls me to see you with a Reynaud."

"You liked this family well enough once." She lowered her voice even though there was no one around as she sidled around a low brick dividing wall laden with thick green vines. "And you raised me to like them, too."

"A little too damn well," he snapped. "But that could work to my advantage. Maybe you can tell me the location of this big royal wedding. Because if you can give me something I can sell to the press and one-up Leon, you could be forgiven for hobnobbing with the Reynauds."

She gasped, hoping he wasn't serious, not even remotely. "I'm appalled. You've got to be kidding. For pity's sake, Dad—"

"Oh, stop it. I really am only kidding. Mostly." In the background of the call, she could hear the running commentary of a football game announcer. No doubt her father was watching game film while his driver navigated traffic. "I'm checking in to see if you can make an announcement to the press that will shut them up about the Marcus Caruthers case. That angle of your relationship with Jean-Pierre is getting a lot of coverage and it's not good for an NFL coach to have his daughter trying cases against players."

Her blood boiled as she paused beside a rose-covered arbor. She tipped her head against the painted wood frame and hoped the scent of roses would calm her. Her father had been even more furious with her than Jean-Pierre had been over that case, insisting that he'd lose his coaching position for allowing his daughter to argue a harassment suit against a player. She'd called BS on that one. Since Marcus didn't play for the Gladiators, there was no conflict of interest. Tatiana had become all the more adamant to take the case as her father became more insistent that she didn't. And after growing up in a house where superstar athletes had always been more important than his daughter, she'd been determined to win the judgment.

Perhaps she'd resisted Jean-Pierre's protests of Marcus's innocence because of that. But bottom line, it had been her job to argue for her client. Yanking a rose off the vine-covered arbor, she charged up the flagstone path toward the house.

"We've had this argument. At length." She stopped in Gervais's driveway to finish her call since she couldn't enter the house while discussing a hot-button topic. "The case is over."

"Not in the eyes of the press, it's not," her father growled at her, his voice forcing her to turn down the volume on her phone. "This is a story all over again, Tatiana, and you can't just bury your head in the sand and pretend it doesn't exist. You stirred the pot by baiting Jean-Pierre with that comment to a reporter. Now you've got to deal with the fallout, and you need to do it before you introduce my grandson to the world."

He was right about that much.

And possibly the part about burying her head in the sand, too. She closed her eyes, willing her heart rate to slow down. She inhaled the scent of the rose she still held crushed in one palm.

"I'll read the headlines and look into a plan of action," she assured him. "I'll do what I can to take care of this. But, Dad?"

"I'm listening."

"If you do anything to detract from this wedding, or in any way upset the Reynauds, you will be alienating me and your grandson, too." Her voice vibrated as she said the words. It was a sign of nervousness but she hoped it came across as an indication of how thoroughly she meant it.

She'd tried to please an impossible taskmaster for too long. Somehow, being a mother gave her fresh perspective on that relationship. And maybe gave her a bit more backbone as well.

"Dammit, honey, I told you I was teasing," he grumbled while a siren wailed on his end of the phone. "Call your mother soon, won't you?"

A deep sigh escaped her as she thought of how easily her mother had always let Dad steamroller them both, never taking Tatiana's side when they disagreed. She loved her mother, but she had vowed to be stronger than that for César. "Of course."

Disconnecting the call, she felt relieved to have drawn a line in the sand with her father. But the news he'd delivered still sucked some of the life out of her on a day that had already started out badly. Reminding herself Marcus Caruthers had been tried in front of a jury of his peers, she shoved the thoughts out of her head to focus on whatever wedding crisis Gervais and Erika were facing. If she'd met the couple under different circumstances, she would have truly enjoyed her evening with them the night before.

Pressing the doorbell, Tatiana barely had time to toss aside the crushed rose before the door swung open. A different maid greeted her in the entryway today. But she was no less efficient. With a smile and gesture, the woman guided Tatiana inside. Tatiana followed her across the marble floors in the opposite direction from the night before.

Her high heels echoed in the wide-open corridors as they passed a library and a feminine-looking office space in the front of the house. Reaching a closed door at the far end, Tatiana could hear music from within—a '70s disco tune. Two female voices were harmonizing the chorus. So far, it didn't sound like a crisis.

The maid knocked briefly on the door and then opened it to admit her to a dimly lit home theater room with deep blue walls and rich, burgundy trim. Wide leather seats faced a screen showing Hurricanes game film, though the sound was turned off. And instead of Gervais and the rest of the family sitting in the chairs, she found all seven of them—including Jean-Pierre—seated on the floor in the open space between the seats and the screen, surrounded by boxes of small wine bottles, stacks of labels and pots of brightly colored paints on a drop cloth.

Someone turned the music down as she neared the group.

Jean-Pierre rose to greet her while the others called out hellos. For the most part, however, they remained focused on their task. Which seemed to be painting labels.

She turned questioningly toward Jean-Pierre, whose presence reminded her in vivid detail of the dreams she'd had about him the night before. Dreams where he'd peeled off all her clothing with slow, tantalizing touches, kissing each inch as he unveiled her...

"Thank you for coming." If he noticed that she felt flustered, he didn't say anything about it. Tucking a hand under her arm, he led her toward the group seated on the floor, the warmth of his hand on her bare skin sending a delicious shiver through her. "Gervais and Erika had a setback with their wedding plans last night and we're helping them out in here because the media room is the most secure room in the house and there seems to have been a privacy breach from someone on staff here."

Tatiana stiffened since her father had only recently suggested she betray the family's privacy. But she knew he would never choose revenge over his own daughter. He might be a self-centered man, but he loved her in his own way.

Erika stopped in midsong to interject. "We're not sure about the breach."

Fiona continued to hum along and paint from where she sat, crossed-legged, on Henri's lap.

Henri reclined against a chair and used Fiona's back as his painting surface, his tongue tucked into his cheek as he gave the project intense concentration. The couple, she realized, never seemed to stop touching each other, which said a lot for their marriage considering they were far from newlyweds.

"It could have been a coincidence," Gervais continued, looking up from his work, which involved centering the dried labels on the wine bottles.

They were wedding favors, she realized, with a personalized message on each bottle for their guests.

"Our wedding planner is ill after traveling to Singapore last week for an event." Erika leaned back from her work, tossing her head so that her thick blond hair almost grazed the floor when she arched her spine to stretch out a kink.

Gervais reached to rub her back for her while Jean-Pierre cleared a spot on the floor for Tatiana to sit. Not an easy task when she'd worn a minidress, but Adelaide seemed to sense her dilemma and handed her a giant pillow.

"For your lap," she whispered as she leaned over.

Gratefully, Tatiana used the pillow to cover her legs.

"The wedding planner obtained the wine for us, but she had a difficult time of it even though we purposely ordered from Gervais's Uncle Michael, who has a vineyard on the West Coast." Erika recounted the tale with her lovely accent that sounded a bit like Swedish; her tiny island country sat off the Finnish coast. "Apparently, there is another family feud that I did not know about." She raised an eyebrow at Gervais.

"I didn't know where you sourced the wine, but I regret the stress it has caused." He spoke to his pregnant bride with a gentleness that made Tatiana's heart feel hollow by comparison.

She glanced at Jean-Pierre beside her, wondering where he'd spent the night after leaving her alone. He looked even more exhausted than she felt, with shadows under his eyes and his face still sporting yesterday's growth of beard. She wondered what it would feel like to run her fingers across his darkened jaw, to kiss the strong column of his neck.

"It is all right. I come from a large family myself. I understand the inevitable disputes." Erika brushed her fingers along Gervais's face in the way Tatiana had just been daydreaming of touching Jean-Pierre.

Did these women know how fortunate they were to have found love that would sustain their hearts as well as their physical needs? Amid so much romance, Tatiana almost found it difficult to breathe. She, of all of them, should have worked out her relationship before she had a child. She regretted for César's sake that she'd failed.

"So your wedding planner obtained the bottles but they didn't come with labels?" Tatiana asked, wanting to help and needing a task before her thoughts drove her mad with wanting and frustration.

"My wedding planner would have helped me with the messages for each bottle. She's very good at this kind of thing and she set aside the next two days to paint the labels personally since the shipment was late and she knows we cannot trust many outsiders with wedding details."

"But then she got ill." Tatiana began to see the problem.

"We have not subcontracted many of the responsibilities for the wedding since the press has been relentless in trying to figure out our plans," Erika continued. "And I really wanted the date and our names on these, so I could hardly ask a local artist to do this without risking helicopter flyovers during my vows." She straightened from her brief break and went back to painting a daisy on a label. "This, I will not have."

Beside her, Jean-Pierre passed her a list of guests' names.

"The rest of us are just filling in the standard information," he explained, showing her several templates. "The whole point is to make each one unique, so you can be creative."

Seeing these men—two of them superstars in the NFL and the other two the power behind the Hurricanes' success—all giving their undivided attention to the preparation of personalized wedding favors would have tugged at her emotions even if she hadn't been vulnerable to bouts of sentimentality lately. The idea of these brothers, who had always been so strong-willed and competitive, all pulling together to provide a happy day for a pregnant princess really got to her.

There was no doubt about it, she wished she'd been able to establish herself within a supportive family situation before the birth of her son. He deserved to have come into the world with this kind of love all around him, as opposed to alone on a Caribbean island with only his mother to welcome him.

She peered around at the work of each of the Reynaud men. She noted the neat black lines on Jean-Pierre's labels, no surprise since he tended to be methodical in football, too, clinically picking apart defenses. Henri chose bold colors and took more chances in his artwork, the same way he did on the field when he chose the long, risky passes that sometimes paid off and sometimes backfired. Dempsey created geometric grid borders, choosing established patterns but filling them in with unexpected colors, which seemed to coincide with an upbringing where he'd had to make up the rules himself since his drug-addicted birth mother had never provided boundaries or safety. And Gervais, the oldest, was probably the most stern and serious of the four, yet his labels were the most unique and fully imagined. One of his starry sky backgrounds suggested he had real artistic talent.

Jean-Pierre dragged over a few pots of watercolors for her while the rest of the family went back to painting and talking, or singing along to the music that someone had turned back up. Adelaide rose from her seat on the other side of Tatiana to grab a bottle of water from a cooler, leaving Jean-Pierre and Tatiana in a bubble of privacy.

"I'm sorry about last night." He sketched his label letters in pencil, using a ruler to be sure of the spacing. "I wish I'd had the presence of mind to talk things through with you then, but I hope we can correct that later today."

Surprised, she picked up her first blank label and thought about what she would create. What would her patterns and colors say about her? She knew one thing. She was done coloring in the lines and making safe choices to please the people around her. Now that she was a mother, she understood that she didn't want her child to have a role model who played it safe all the time. She dipped a brush into a pot of bright orange paint.

"A discussion would probably be wise." She knew without question that he wanted what was best for César. Jean-Pierre's love for his child had been evident almost immediately in the tender way he held him. After seeing the way he behaved with his son, she wondered how she could have doubted him during her pregnancy. But she'd had her reasons at the time. She could only move forward now. "My father called this morning to alert me to the media's renewed interest in the Caruthers case. I didn't realize it had come back to life, but I do want to think about how to deflect interest away from that if at all possible."

"Good." Setting aside his pencil, he watched her for a long moment as she painted a starburst border on her first label. "I want to do whatever it takes to find some common ground this week. I am fully committed."

Something in his tone made her pause. She moved the brush away from the label so as not to spoil her work.

One look into Jean-Pierre's dark eyes told her he meant it. There was a depth of sincerity there that she would guess he didn't let many people see. She herself hadn't seen it in years. But she remembered that expression from long, long ago.

And it had much the same effect on her now that it'd had then. Her heart fluttered. Sped up. Made her breathless.

"That sounds…" Her voice hitched and she cleared her throat, trying to banish runaway thoughts of what it might be like to have this man fully committed to her. Even just for the rest of the week. Even for just one more night. "That is, I agree."

She licked her lips and went back to the label, blinking away the chemistry that had always hit her so hard with him.

"Need some cold water?" Adelaide asked her, suddenly appearing beside her with an extra bottle from the cooler.

You have no idea, she thought.

"Thank you." She took it gratefully, hoping that she could turn down the temperature of her heated skin with a drink. But no such luck.

His low chuckle suggested he hadn't missed her reaction.

Having Jean-Pierre working silently beside her called to her senses, making her wish she could climb into his lap the way Fiona did with Henri. Or that he would steal a kiss when he thought no one was looking, the way she'd seen Dempsey do with Adelaide.

But the most she could hope for—and all that Jean-Pierre really wanted—was to find some kind of mental common ground where they could agree on how to raise César together in a way that would help their son to thrive.

She wanted that, too. And yet…how nice it would have been to have something more. Some sense that he would throw logic and caution to the wind and take a chance on a deeper connection than carefully agreed on terms for parenting.

"Before I forget," Gervais said suddenly, turning down the music again. "I've chartered two flights on Saturday for wedding guests who arrive here thinking the wedding is still taking place in Louisiana. But the family will relocate to the island early to settle in before the ceremony. Leon and his nurse will leave in the morning, so he'll meet us there. Can everyone else be ready to depart tomorrow evening?"

While the group fine-tuned travel arrangements, Jean-Pierre's gaze connected with hers. Perhaps he sensed her apprehension at seeing Leon again. The Reynaud family patriarch had been the one to fire her father and turn her life upside down, effectively ending the young romance she'd apparently never gotten over.

"Will your grandfather keep César a secret from the press?" she ventured aloud to Jean-Pierre, unsure how much longer they would be able to keep their son out of the media storm swirling around the Reynauds lately.

"We should probably talk about that." He slid a hand onto her knee beneath the pillow on her lap. But his expression was serious. He seemed to be touching her to steady her more than anything. "Leon has Alzheimer's and can't keep a secret of any kind. He's been blurting out information from the past and nothing's sacred with him because he can't remember what to keep quiet about."

"I'm sorry to hear that," she said quickly, genuinely saddened to learn of his health problems. She couldn't stop herself from touching Jean-Pierre's hand lightly. "I know this must hurt you. I wish César could have the chance to know him better before…well. It's just such a tragic disease. I'm not sure what to say or how to handle things. It could complicate the announcement about César."

"I know." Jean-Pierre's thumb shifted on the inside of her knee, a tiny movement that sent a bolt of awareness through her whole body. "All the more reason we need a plan for how to reveal him to the press so we control the story."

"Right." She agreed wholeheartedly.

The problem was, neither of them seemed to have any idea what that story might be. Because the only thing she understood for certain about her relationship with Jean-Pierre right now was that she couldn't go on denying the chemistry that all but set her on fire every time he was near.

Besides, she'd been to see a local doctor this morning and obtained her official six-week clearance for intimacy. Just thinking about it made her stomach flutter with nerves—and excitement. She couldn't deny she still wanted Jean-Pierre.

Even thinking about his grandfather's illness made her realize what a short window of time she had here to make some life-altering decisions. This could well be her last chance to indulge in this tenacious attraction.

Maybe, in this frustrating search for common ground, they needed to revisit the one place they'd always found it—in each other's arms.

Nine

Jean-Pierre checked his watch at seven o'clock the next evening as the limo dropped him and Tatiana, as well as César and his nanny, off at the private airport close to the family compound. The party of four had arrived early to give Tatiana a little extra time to settle the baby. She had delayed the morning feeding so he could nurse during takeoff. She hoped to ease César's transition into the air since small children often felt the effects of the change in air pressure as pain in the ears. Apparently, the act of suckling relieved that pressure. That she'd researched this before the flight impressed Jean-Pierre, giving him yet another reason to admire her parenting.

He'd begun to think that the best way to convince her to say yes to his marriage proposal was to demonstrate his value to her as a father. But beyond naming the child heir to a fortune, he was still looking for ways to make his potential contributions more apparent.

Now, he passed a fussing César into Lucinda's arms while he helped Tatiana from the vehicle. Their driver had already taken charge of the luggage, so they were able to board after an exchange of pleasantries with the pilot, a man who'd flown Jean-Pierre back and forth to New York on numerous occasions.

He hoped the man proved as trustworthy as he'd always thought him to be because allowing him to observe Tatiana and César in Jean-Pierre's company amounted to giving him one hell of a valuable headline. But after considerable discussion the day before, he and Tatiana had agreed it would be best to bring César to Texas with them. She was breast-feeding almost exclusively, for one thing. And for another, Jean-Pierre found he didn't want to lose any time with his son after missing those early weeks of the child's life. Besides, if he was going to prove his value to Tatiana as a father, it would help to keep his son close at hand and learn more about this little life they'd made together.

Even if the boy's presence made it a challenge to get time with her alone.

"Where should we sit?" she asked as they boarded the empty plane.

The Gulfstream had been designed for business more than pleasure, but there were a few different seat configurations to choose from. Jean-Pierre pointed to seats in the back.

"It will be most private back here." He escorted her to two seats positioned side by side. "There's a privacy screen that's meant for sleeping, but I can lower that for you, too."

Lucinda passed César back to him before taking another chair on the opposite side of the plane and withdrawing a book from her bag.

Peering down at his son's wriggling form, his tiny mouth seeking food as his head turned this way and that,

Jean-Pierre experienced a rush of protectiveness so fierce it damn near floored him.

"I'm ready," he heard Tatiana say behind him, reminding him he had a role to play, too. "I don't want the baby to have to wait much longer. And we should be taking off soon."

Would he be able to continue playing football at the level he maintained now? Somehow he didn't think his focus would ever be the same again. Traveling across the country with Tatiana and César in tow wouldn't allow him to spend the same amount of time on his game preparation, which some sportswriters suggested was actually his strongest asset as an athlete. His mental game. What Henri had always managed through God-given talent and instinct, Jean-Pierre manufactured through sheer will and study.

"Jean-Pierre?" Tatiana called to him. "I can take him."

Turning to see her with her simple sundress already sliding off one creamy shoulder, his thoughts shifted from his son to the boy's mother so fast he felt dizzy.

She'd brought a soft purple cashmere sweater to rest on her shoulders. The line of pearl buttons followed her curves in a way that made his mouth go dry.

Lowering himself to sit beside her, he tugged down the privacy screen beside his seat, shrouding them in relative intimacy. His eyes never left her body—so beautiful, but so much more than that—as she reached to take César and cradle him to her breast.

Speechless at the sight of her, Jean-Pierre couldn't wait to get to Texas so they could be alone. To lay claim to her as his in a way he hadn't been able to the only time they'd shared a bed. Being with her now would be so much different than it had been ten months ago.

"We're sharing a room on the island," he announced in the hands-down worse segue of his life.

Of course, if she could have followed his thoughts, it would have made perfect sense.

"I understand." She brushed a dark curl away from her face, revealing an earring with a simple diamond stud in her ear. "I know the ranch is not a hotel. I'm just glad to have a place to stay."

The fact that she hadn't protested the arrangement encouraged him. Since their blowup the first night at Gervais's, they both seemed to tread a bit more cautiously. And, perhaps, respectfully. They had too much at stake to risk alienating one another.

"Lucinda will share a room with César next door, but you might speak with her about the importance of remaining within her quarters as much as possible for security purposes." He worried about what a leak to the press might do at this stage of their relationship. "We have weathered enough media scrutiny and conjecture for one week."

Outside the plane, he could hear the others arriving and more luggage being stowed beneath the passenger cabin. As the first of their party boarded, he could hear the nanny explaining to someone—Fiona, he thought—that Tatiana was feeding César.

That would save him from having to greet his family for now. He'd far rather watch Tatiana nurse his son. He leaned closer to brush her hair from her shoulder, out of the way of César's clutching hand. The boy seemed to meet his gaze over the high curve of Tatiana's breast. Jean-Pierre gave the baby one of his fingers to grip instead.

The action had been instinctual, sure. But as soon as he did it, he realized how the movement put his palm mere inches from Tatiana's other breast. Still tucked safely in her dress, the soft curve called to him anyhow. This close to her, he caught the scent of her fragrance, something clean and lemony that made him hunger to find its source.

Behind an ear? Along the slender column of her neck?

"Jean-Pierre?" she whispered suddenly, her voice containing an unexpected hint of urgency while his family found seats scattered around the luxury jet.

"What is it? Do you need anything?" Had she forgotten some necessity back at the house? Even now the door was closing to the passenger cabin, the pilot warning them to strap in for the flight.

"No. It's not—" She bit her lip, her green gaze sliding higher to meet his. He could see the heat there. The hunger. "You shouldn't look at me like that in public places."

Understanding dawned. And with it came a need so strong he debated carrying her off the plane and finding the nearest hotel room. He might have done it, too, if not for César.

In fact he had done something just like that nearly a year ago when they'd created their child.

"The flight is blessedly short. And we have a good excuse for retreating directly to our suite since we have an infant to care for." And then another thought occurred to him. "Although we need to wait until you see a physician—"

"I did. Yesterday morning before we worked on the wine-bottle labels. That's why I was late to Gervais's house." She lowered her window shade as the plane began to taxi toward the short runway.

"You saw a local doctor?" He pried his finger from the baby's grip, regretting not being there with her for that visit. She must have gone out while he'd been recovering from the midnight workout at the Hurricanes' training facility. "Is everything…okay?"

The barest hint of a smile teased her lips. "I'm cleared to resume normal activity, if that's what you mean."

He sure as hell couldn't miss what she implied.

Heat scorched its way up his spine as the plane fired faster. His pulse kicked up speed, too, not just because of the green light she'd received from an obstetrician, but also from the green light he spied in her eyes.

For him.

"I care about more than that, Tatiana." He cradled her cheek in his hand as the aircraft lifted off. "I am so grateful you are healthy and that you did a beautiful thing in delivering our son. But I'd be lying if I said I wasn't extremely interested in touching you. Everywhere."

Her slow swallow intrigued him. She cleared her throat and then asked, "How long did you say the flight lasts?"

The flight went as quickly as Jean-Pierre had said it would. But the pilot couldn't land on the island so they needed to ferry over from Galveston. Or, rather, the pilot could have landed on the Reynauds' private island off the Texas gulf coast, but Gervais hadn't wanted to draw that kind of attention to the wedding destination since the family's every movement was being scrutinized. Bodyguards traveled with them now. Decoy limos had left the family compound at intervals all day to confuse the members of the media who'd set up camp outside the gates to the houses on Lake Pontchartrain.

A Reynaud wedding garnered attention. A Reynaud wedding to a royal made for a media circus.

So the trip to the island was purposely a bit longer than necessary to throw story seekers off their scent, which was a good thing for César's sake as well as protecting the wedding secret. The private ferry ride from Galveston to the island went smoothly enough. As they reached the dock on the western side of the land mass, Tatiana wished it was daylight so she could appreciate the lay of the land.

She hugged the rail of the boat while the others began

debarking. Lucinda held César, who was fast asleep. But Tatiana didn't feel even the smallest bit tired after her electrifying conversation with the man standing next to her. Her body still hummed with anticipation from just a few simple words.

He'd said he wanted to touch her. Everywhere.

His eyes had communicated his desires far more explicitly, however. And all the pent-up hunger she felt coursed through her tenfold.

If they salvaged nothing else from their relationship, they would have César. And they would have tonight.

"Ready?" Jean-Pierre asked, extending a hand. The lights from the dock behind him cast his features in shadow, but made him appear all the larger.

If any paparazzi surprised them, she thought she would be able to hide behind his broad shoulders easily.

"Very." She laid her palm against his for a moment before interlacing their fingers, locking them together.

"I'll introduce you to my cousin Kimberly, then I'll see about getting you and César both settled for the night."

She wanted to press herself into him and kiss him, then and there. Remind him that she didn't want to be settled. That what she wanted was to have his arms around her, sifting through her hair and parting the zipper on her dress. She wanted to take chances and throw caution to the humid Texas wind.

"That sounds good." Realistically, she knew she didn't have to wait much longer to touch him. But she didn't know how she'd make it through much more social chitchat. To distract herself from the kiss she wanted, she asked him about his relatives. "Tell me about the Texas Reynauds. How come I never met any of your cousins when I visited your family at the big ranch?"

Memories of the endless spread of hill country returned.

There had been long afternoons of hiking trails or horse-back riding, nighttime picnics under the stars, and the heady pleasure of being the only girl with four handsome older boys to keep her entertained. Before they'd grown older and started to pursue their own interests, leaving her to Jean-Pierre's care, her ten-year-old self had been a little in love with them all.

"My grandfather, Leon, did a great job stepping in to raise my brothers and me after our parents divorced. But the reason Leon worked hard to get it right with us is because he screwed up his own sons so thoroughly. His words, not mine, by the way." Jean-Pierre's gaze followed Lucinda, his sharp eyes missing nothing as she stepped into a waiting golf cart with César and they sped off toward the looming ranch house in the distance.

Gervais commandeered a small luxury bus for the rest of them while giving instructions for the luggage. Tatiana admired that no matter how wealthy and powerful the man was, he still oversaw details himself, taking no chances with his pregnant wife or his family.

"Leon blames himself for his sons' shortcomings? Keep in mind, I don't know anything about your uncles and I've only met your father a few times." She'd only spoken to Theo Reynaud once, at a long-ago birthday party for one of the boys. The man had touched down by helicopter, stayed long enough to have a few drinks and departed with his latest girlfriend within the hour.

Tatiana had been decidedly unimpressed.

Following Jean-Pierre toward the waiting vehicle, she noticed Adelaide tucked under Dempsey's arm as they sat on a bench on the dock, her eyes closed as she tipped her head against his chest. Fiona and Henri were quiet, too, talking softly in the back of the bus when Tatiana entered with Jean-Pierre. So it didn't feel rude to continue their own conversation while the family boarded.

"Leon thought it would make his sons tougher to pit them against each other." Jean-Pierre slid into a leather captain's chair midway up one aisle of the bus. He reached up to turn off the reading lamp above the seat, plunging them into darkness before he tugged her closer, wrapping an arm around her waist. "He started rivalries when they were young, pushing them to outdo one another on the football field and on the ranch since he was based in Texas back then. Once, a bull-riding contest between them nearly killed my Uncle Michael."

"That's awful." She relaxed against him, her cheek pressed to the hard muscle of his chest, his body warming her.

She felt the slow thud of his heartbeat beneath her ear and she couldn't resist laying her hand on him, feeling the hard ridges of muscles in his abdomen beneath the thin cotton of his shirt.

He responded by stroking her hair away from her face. A gentle gesture that might appear sweet to a casual observer, but the sensual heat it roused was enough to set her on fire.

"Eventually, Christophe, Michael and my father cut all personal ties and moved to different states. But since the shipping empire is still a family business, they are bound together professionally." He nodded to Gervais as his brother boarded with his fiancée. The couple took the front seat behind the driver and signaled him to begin the short trip to the main house while Jean-Pierre wound up his family primer for her. "Kimberly, who we'll meet when we get to the house, is one of Christophe's daughters. She doesn't get along with her father, either, but she deals with him well enough that he lets her run this place. The island ranch is a self-sustaining subsidiary of the main ranching operation and also a stop on many of our cruise ships' Gulf of Mexico itineraries."

Tatiana lifted her head from her comfortable position to peer up at him. "You're such a successful athlete, I forget that you have a whole other side to you as an heir to the family's business."

"It's a lot to keep up with since the company interests are so diverse, but considering the short career of an NFL athlete, I know that the business will keep me employed long after football is done with me."

The luxury bus hit a pothole and pitched enough to one side that she fell against him again. Not that she minded. And from the way his eyes glittered in the dim lights outlining the walkway on the floor, she'd guess he didn't mind, either.

"You're only a year older than me," she teased, smoothing a hand along his shoulder and upper arm to grip his biceps. "I think you've got a few years left in your arm."

"If I'm lucky," he said, in all seriousness. "Injuries can happen at any time in the game. I don't count on a paycheck from the Gladiators or any other team, but no matter what my future is in football, rest assured our son will be well provided for. Always."

"I don't want to think about you being hurt." She closed her eyes tight, knowing he spoke the truth. She'd been around football long enough to understand the dangers, to see young, vital men halted in their athletic careers because of irreversible damage that decreased their speed or mobility.

"I'm a realist. I account for as many possibilities as I can foresee, and that's a skill that has served me well." His hand slid beneath the collar of her cashmere sweater to massage the bare skin of her shoulder. "But I can honestly say César was an outcome I never accounted for and I should have. I'm sorry about that, Tatiana."

The soft words, spoken into her hair as the bus slowed to a stop, caught her off guard. She hadn't expected him to apologize for not checking in with her after that explosive encounter ten and a half months ago, but she appreciated the thought nevertheless.

"We were careful at the time. You had no reason to suspect—"

"It's always a possibility." The brusque statement left no room for argument. "I should have called afterward, when I'd cooled down…" She sensed a hesitation. As if he didn't want to confide whatever he was thinking.

And he didn't.

Instead, he straightened, bringing her with him. As they followed his brothers and their significant others from the vehicle, Tatiana shoved aside her troubled thoughts so she could meet their hostess.

The Tides Ranch was a massive complex with a central hacienda-style adobe main house that glowed a bronze shade of pink in the landscape lights. Native plantings on terraced beds hinted at the ranch's self-sustaining practices, as did the solar panels on the roofs, evident even in the dark from the way they glinted in the moonlight. Although Tatiana had read that the ranch housed some of the owner's family year-round, the front entrance had the feel of a hotel, complete with a staffed front desk, since the island received a high number of annual visitors thanks to being a stop for cruise ships.

Warm mesquite wood furnishings and Saltillo tile floors enhanced the Southwest appeal of the house. Exposed beam ceilings and bright woven rugs drew her eye toward a large entertaining space, a family room that looked as though it would hold sixty people easily.

"Welcome to the Tides." A willowy blonde with cool gray eyes appeared in the reception area as they entered, opening her arms to Gervais and each of the Reynaud brothers in turn, then greeting the women briefly. "I can't tell you how thrilled I am to host a wedding this weekend instead of our usual tourists," she said, squeezing Erika's hand warmly. "Not that we don't appreciate all our visitors, of course. But it will be fun to take our level of entertaining up a notch. As a foreign princess, your options for wedding sites must have been limitless."

Tatiana knew how tired Erika was by that time, having recently survived her own narcoleptic second trimester. And she hadn't even been pregnant with twins. But looking at the bride-to-be, you'd never guess she had fallen asleep on Gervais's shoulder on the short bus trip from the dock to the ranch house.

"Come on." Jean-Pierre spoke into her ear, tugging her away from the conversation. "I grabbed our key from the desk. Kimberly knows about the baby. She'll understand."

He tossed a brief "good night and thank you" over his shoulder as he pulled Tatiana toward the back of the main building. Her kitten heels clicked on the Saltillo tiles, her hand warm in his as he drew her up a short staircase decorated with Spanish tile mosaic. They walked out into a breezeway open to the elements, cloister-style. He paused outside a dark wooden door decorated with a blue-and-yellow tile motif that matched the card on the old-fashioned key he carried.

Hearing it click into place in the lock made her temperature spike, the sound an audible reminder of what was to come with the utter privacy behind that door.

"Should I check on César?" she asked, peering around the corridor as if she could guess what room he might be in.

"Why don't you let me. I'll give you some privacy to

get settled while I make sure Lucinda has the baby's bags and we have ours." He pushed open the door and held it for her. "I'll get a baby monitor, too, so we can hear him tonight if he needs to be fed."

"Okay." She nodded, a nervous laugh escaping. "Is it strange to plan for baby care the second time we ever share a…um, romantic evening?"

"No." He drew her into the room with him, letting the door fall shut behind them. A small wrought-iron chandelier in the foyer area flickered to life on a dim setting as they entered. He stood, centered under that chandelier, and reeled her toward him. Closer. Closer. Until she was toe-to-toe with him. Breasts-to-chest. "It seems like everything I've wanted since I first saw you holding our son that night in New York is about to come true." His hands clamped her forearms, holding her still. His voice dipped lower as he tipped her chin up with one finger. "It feels perfect."

Nervousness faded. Her pulse hammered faster as sensations skidded along her spine, tension coiling deep within her.

When his mouth finally brushed hers, she thought she'd faint from the sheer pleasure of it. The warm slide of his lips was a sensual treat for a woman who'd had little enough romantic attention in the last year. The bay-rum-and-sandalwood scent of his aftershave teased her nose, calling her to taste his skin, but Jean-Pierre had taken full command of the kiss by then.

Her head spun as he raised his hand to either side of her face, bracketing her jaw and tilting her chin to just the right angle. Her knees wobbled, her body seized with the need to melt into him. A moan simmered up her throat but didn't escape, his kiss consuming it. His fingers sifted into her hair, sending tantalizing warmth along the base of her scalp even as shivers tingled along her nerve endings.

She would have fallen into him completely if he hadn't pulled away just then. As he glanced down at her, his breath came fast, his chest moving up and down as though he'd been sprinting.

"Hold that thought." He kissed her hard on the lips, like a warrior leaving to do battle instead of a new father retrieving a nursery monitor. But feeling the way she did, she could completely appreciate where he was coming from because pulling away from that kiss took a whole lot of grit and resolve, almost more than she could manage right now. "I'll be right back."

As he strode out of their suite, she hoped he would hurry.

If this trip was the only time they had together, she wanted it to be perfect.

Ten

He only left the room for fifteen minutes to tuck in César.

Jean-Pierre kissed his sleeping son's head, ensured the baby and his nanny had everything they needed and then double-checked the status of their bags. Because he didn't want someone knocking on his door in half an hour to deliver them, he waited just long enough to secure the luggage personally and have it brought up with him. Impatient as hell, he tipped the young man generously to make sure they weren't disturbed until he called downstairs, but he put in an advance order with the kitchen to have a few of Tatiana's favorites ready upon request later.

After a deep bracing breath, he opened the door to the bedroom he would be sharing with Tatiana.

The air left his lungs twice as fast.

Considering how briefly he'd left the room, he was surprised at the transformation when he returned. Not that he'd devoted even two seconds checking out the décor when they'd arrived. He'd been too busy trying not to devour Tatiana whole.

But when he'd been in the suite before, there hadn't been any seductive Spanish guitar music gently playing from hidden speakers. And he wouldn't have missed candlelight flickering through the open archway that led to the bedroom. The warm golden glow was the only thing that illuminated the space, though a smaller candle burned on top of the wet bar close to the entrance. The windows had been thrown open—though the heavy wooden blinds remaining closed—so that a fresh gulf breeze drifted through the slats, gently stirring the sheer white curtains draping the corners of a wrought-iron four-poster bed.

He could see the bed now as he was drawn deeper into the suite to see what other surprises the night—and Tatiana—had in store.

"I hope you don't mind the candles." Tatiana emerged from behind a decorative screen made of colorful serapes that had been stretched to fit tall, rectangular frames.

Her feet were bare, her beautiful dark hair loose around her shoulders as she brushed it, one slow seductive sweep at a time. She wore a white linen nightgown that bared her shoulders and just covered her knees. He'd seen her wear something just like it once before, when he'd thrown stones at her bedroom window as a teenager to get her attention and she'd opened the sash to lean out.

He couldn't decide if seeing her this way was like seeing his teenage fantasy come to life.

Or like taking a bride to his bed.

Both thoughts rattled him, but for far different reasons. "Tatiana?"

"You have to ask?" She laughed softly, setting aside the silver-backed hairbrush, although she didn't step any closer. "I can switch on a real light if you need one. It's just that candlelight is a postpartum woman's best friend. More flattering, you know?" she rambled, obviously nervous. "My body has been through a lot since the last time you saw it."

Ruthlessly, he tamped down his own lust to dial into what she was saying.

"You look so damn beautiful I can't even find words," he said and meant it. Every. Damn. Word.

He took a step toward her, the movement so carefully measured he probably looked like a robot.

But it was that, or risk a diving tackle that would get them both horizontal as fast as possible and…yeah. Not happening. He needed to remember she'd had a baby recently. And yes, he wanted to savor every moment of being with her again.

Another step brought him close enough to touch her. He skimmed a light caress up her arms, circling around the tops of her shoulders and slipping his thumbs just barely under the wide straps of the nightgown until a shiver ran through her.

"Thank you for understanding." She lifted her palms to his chest and smoothed them down the front of his shirt. She hesitated at the bottom, but soon she walked two fingers beneath the fabric to hook into the waistband of his trousers. "It's hard to think about being with you when you work so hard to hone and refine your body every day for football and I just—"

"You used yours for the most important thing in the world. No comparison." He wasn't even listening to that line of discussion. His touch fell to her belly through the soft linen. "If we'd been together while César grew inside you, I would have told you every day how amazing you were to do that. And I am certain you were every bit as beautiful."

Her lips curved in a smile, bringing a sparkle to her green eyes.

"But since we weren't together during those months—" she arched up on her toes to whisper in his ear "—I've had a long time to miss your touch."

A groan vibrated through him, the hunger tougher to restrain when she said things like that. Especially now that her palm raked over his abs and around to the small of his back, and delectable breasts pressed against his chest.

Seized by the need to lie with her, he plucked her off her feet and cradled her in his arms, carrying her to the high bed. He climbed onto the soft down mattress, the feather stuffing flattening under his knees as he shifted his weight to make her more comfortable.

He wanted to take his time. To square the pillow beneath her head and smooth her hair from her shoulders. To breathe kisses along her collarbone and up the creamy arch of her neck. But she was already making quick work of the buttons on his shirt, skimming the fabric off his shoulders until he had no choice but to ease it to the floor beside the bed.

"We have to go slow," he reminded her. "Be careful."

"I can't go slow." She shook her head, sending dark curls wriggling on the pale sheets. "I need you. I need this."

"I don't want to hurt you." Grinding his teeth as she pressed a kiss along his jaw, he hoped he had the fortitude to ensure he was careful with her.

Six weeks ago she'd delivered a baby. And although she looked more beautiful than ever, and she'd kissed him with enough heat to scorch the sheets, he would make damn sure he took care of her.

"You won't hurt me." She twisted her leg so that her foot stroked up his calf, the movement causing her thigh to shift against his, her hips cradling the hard length of him against her softness.

"Tatiana." He had to close his eyes against another heated rush of longing. Hunger.

"Please," she whispered in his ear, nipping the lobe before she licked it with a deft swipe of her tongue. "For a little while, I just want to be a woman and not a mother."

Her confession called to the most elemental need and he tunneled his hands beneath the nightgown to touch her naked body. Hips, waist, breasts. He reacquainted himself with her curves in long, possessive strokes over her skin.

The touch unleashed something in her, a reserve that she was only too glad to set aside, her kisses growing more fevered.

Rolling her on top of him, he skimmed the gown up and off of her, her dark hair falling all around him and veiling their kiss in curls. He cupped her breasts, heavier than they'd been the last time, but the tips tightened just the way he remembered.

With the lemony scent of her hair in his nose and the golden glow of candlelight flickering over her creamy skin, he could have explored her body all night long. But he didn't want to wear her out. Instead, he flipped her to her back on the thick feather bed and proceeded to give her what she'd asked for.

Because it would be his intense pleasure to make her feel like a woman.

"Jean-Pierre?" Tatiana blinked up at him as he stretched out over her, his powerful body making her feel tiny beneath him despite the extra weight the pregnancy had left behind.

Shirtless, he was a mouthwatering sight. But the fact that his mouth trailed kisses lower and lower down her newly curvier body made her self-conscious no matter what he spouted about her beauty. Her stretch marks looked like white vines had a stranglehold on her hips.

"Too late to change your mind," he warned her, his breath fanning over her belly as he spoke. "I'm on a mission."

His tongue swirled into the hollow of her navel, sending pleasurable shivers across her skin along with a rush of heat between her legs. Even seeing his strong shoulders pinning her thighs to the bed was enough to hurtle her affection-starved body toward release.

"I didn't know you would embrace the task so, er... wholeheartedly." She'd had visions of the missionary position. Lovely, fulfilling visions where she could simply close her eyes and lose herself in the feel of all that male strength around and inside her. "Did I mention I'm feeling self-conscious?"

He trailed kisses to one hip and then the other, peering up at her with dark eyes as he licked her. Thoroughly.

"For a little while tonight, you're not a mother." He parroted her words, punctuating them with a kiss on the waistband of her simple cotton bikini panties. "You're a sexy, tantalizing woman." His teeth latched onto the elastic enough to edge them lower on her hip, before his hands slid them off completely. "My woman."

The kiss centered between her thighs was her undoing.

A gasp caught in her throat, the feel of his mouth administering wicked pleasure an experience too good to be tainted with hesitation. Her eyes slid closed, her body melting at his touch. His kiss.

She lost herself utterly, her brain latching on to the sensation of his fingers gripping her hips and his mouth teasing a response from her body faster than she would have imagined possible.

Her release hit her hard, coming in wave after wave of

pleasure. He cupped her with his palm, capturing her release and helping her to ride out each heady spasm.

By the time she dared to slide open her eyes, he was already off the bed and undressing the rest of the way. Grateful she hadn't missed the sight of him naked, she savored the burnished gold of his muscles in the candlelight, his back tapering to narrow hips and strong thighs.

Reaching a languid hand out to touch him, she met his dark gaze and shivered anew. The satisfaction that weighted her limbs and curled in her belly was a release he hadn't found yet—a release he'd delayed for her sake. Even as she appreciated his restraint, she wanted desperately to distract him from his methodical seduction. He deserved the kind of passion that had taken hold of them ten and a half months ago like a fever in their blood.

Infused with new purpose, she levered herself up on an elbow and then to her knees, shuffling over to the edge of the bed where he stood. The glitter of frank male interest in his eyes gratified her, his gaze traveling all over her more generous curves in a way that gave her as much confidence as she could have ever wanted. She twined her arms around his neck and aligned their bodies again, her breasts molding to the hard planes of his pectorals.

With a growl of approval, he banded his arms around her, fitting them together tighter. Harder. Her heart rate sped up as the kiss became more demanding, his fingers spearing into her hair to cup the back of her head, angling her to receive the lush thrust of his tongue.

Lowering her to the bed, he followed her down, one hard thigh claiming the space between hers. He took a condom from the nightstand; he must have left it there when he shed his clothes.

"I've got it." Peering out of the corner of her eye, she took the condom from him. "I don't want you to stop touching me for even a second." Fingers fumbling, she opened the foil package and reached to roll the condom into place.

"Wait." He manacled her wrist with an immovable grip, surprising her. "Your touch could be the end of me." Releasing his hold, he took the condom back. "Let me."

Touched to learn she could affect him like that—this man who had groupies, for pity's sake—she caressed his bristle-roughened jaw and peered into his eyes once he had the protection in place.

Tenderness for him, for all that they'd shared, filled her chest. There'd been a time when she'd been certain she'd lose her virginity to him. A time when she'd dreamed of it in detail—repeatedly.

"Are you okay?" His question brought her back to the moment. Unwilling to let her runaway emotions spoil this, she brushed his dark hair from his forehead.

"I'll be better with you inside me," she told him honestly, needing more of the fulfillment only he could bring.

His gaze narrowed, becoming heavy-lidded with sensual focus. Lowering his mouth to her breast, he teased one tight peak with slow, circling kisses while his fingers dipped between her thighs to play in the slick heat he found there.

Her throaty moan must have encouraged him because he wasted no time positioning himself between her legs. He whispered seductive encouragement in her ear, cradling her close as he entered her. But she felt too good to go slow and, arching her hips, took more of him.

He exercised that iron grip again, holding her there for a long moment, but whether it was for his sake or her own, she couldn't say. All she knew was that it felt perfect, sharing her body with him and sharing this undeniable heat and chemistry that had never really died between them.

Eventually, he moved within her, finding a rhythm that

drove them both to the brink and beyond. As she hurtled toward release, she felt him find his, the hot surge of him inside her driving her higher.

The moment went on and on as they clutched each other in the big feather bed, clinging until every last wave of pleasure had been exhausted. Only then did they fall into each other's arms in the candlelight, allowing the cool gulf breeze to soothe their overheated bodies.

They didn't speak much, but the way he stroked his hand up and down her spine made her feel cherished even if he would never say such a thing. Here, in this bed, there was a connection they'd never been able to form anywhere else.

For now, she didn't want to jinx it. Didn't want to wake up and find that they were back to being at odds again. So with her head tucked against Jean-Pierre's chest, she closed her eyes and wished the night didn't have to end.

Eleven

Two days later, Tatiana was as nervous as a bride and it wasn't even *her* wedding.

The Mitras royal family had arrived at the Tides Ranch the day before, to much fanfare since even the employees of the Reynaud family—who'd seen plenty of celebrities come and go at their elite homes all over the world—were not immune to the draw of royalty. Despite confidentiality agreements and strict rules governing their conduct, everyone from ranch hands to caterers had cell phones out to record the procession of platinum-haired princesses and their elegant parents.

A king and queen.

Tatiana had watched from her suite's private balcony the day before. Curled in Jean-Pierre's lap while César snoozed in a bassinet nearby, she'd been tempted to snap some photos herself.

She had refrained then, but she'd given in to the impulse

to capture a few candids the morning of the wedding while she assisted with last-minute preparations. She'd been helping Jean-Pierre's cousin Kimberly thread bright red hibiscus flowers into a graceful willow arch that would frame the bride and groom during their vows when she'd noticed one of the island's luxury buses rumbling past with wedding guests newly flown in. Unlike the Reynauds, these newest arrivals had landed directly on the island's runway since Gervais and Erika had decided they didn't need the same kind of privacy safeguards this close to the event.

It was too late now. No paparazzi photographer would have the resources to follow the Reynaud private planes before the ceremony began.

"I can't imagine marrying royalty," Kimberly remarked as she dragged over another bucket of hibiscus blooms.

Tatiana had noticed in their short stay that the woman was a hands-on manager of the property, as comfortable greeting guests and riding horses as she was feeding the goats that provided natural weed control on the self-sustaining eco-island. Tatiana admired her commitment to this being an environmentally friendly ranch, right down to the solar-powered cell-phone tower.

"Really?" She stepped back and took a photo of their handiwork to see how it looked on camera. "I always think of the Reynauds as a sort of American royalty, between the wealth, the global connections and the fame."

Kimberly laughed while Tatiana studied her photos and made adjustments.

"Seriously?" The other woman shook her head, peering over Tatiana's shoulder to see how the arch looked on the screen. "I guess the Texas Reynauds are less famous because we don't play football. And since I spend most of my time negotiating with stubborn goats as opposed to negotiating big business deals, I guess I don't see myself as more than a rancher's daughter." Squinting at the thumbnail images on Tatiana's phone, Kimberly pointed to one. "Can I see the rest of your pictures? Some of those Hurricane players are so cute."

"Sure." She passed the device to Jean-Pierre's cousin and straightened a few of the chairs set up for the outdoor ceremony. "But you are far too modest, Kimberly. Anyone can see you make an incredible contribution to the family's cruise ship business by having the Tides as a featured stop on the itineraries. You keep the tourist dollars coming, plus you have an opportunity to educate a huge number of people on the advantages of eco-farming. That must be fulfilling."

"My father doesn't see it that way." Kimberly lowered herself to one of the folding chairs decorated with a length of ice-blue tulle. "He doesn't care about the dollars that funnel into the cruise ship business. He just sees the Tides as a sorry excuse for a ranch compared to the five-thousand-acre spread he oversees."

Tatiana rolled her eyes sympathetically. "That I can empathize with. My father is more interested in my contribution to my law firm's billable hours than my happiness." With a pang, she realized how little he'd said to her about the birth of her son. And while she realized it had been a shock to him at the time, she would have appreciated a call or a note since then.

One that wasn't focused on her plans to keep César hidden from the media for a little while longer.

"Tatiana?" Kimberly seemed to be enlarging one of the images as she stared at it. "Can you take a look at this?"

"Sure." She sat down on the closest chair. Already dressed for the wedding, she rearranged her skirts around her. Her lemon-colored princess-cut gown was strapless and highlighted with tiny yellow sequins in a subtle sunburst pattern. It looked as if a sun glowed from the area of her waist. "Did you find a cute player you want to dance with?"

"I thought I recognized this woman, actually." She pointed to a figure under one of the rookie Hurricane players' arms. "Not all of the guests' names were on my list since many of the wedding attendees were bringing a plus-one that might not be a wife."

Her gaze settled on the person in question. A female a bit blurred from having the photo stretched as large as possible. But Tatiana had captured her as she exited the limo and strode toward the Tides' main building. She must have missed seeing the woman at the time of the photo, her eye focusing on someone or something else in the excitement of the new arrivals.

Yet she recognized her former client very well. Blair Jones was the woman she'd helped sue Marcus Caruthers for sexual harassment. And now, here was Blair, attending a Reynaud wedding with another football player when the Reynaud brothers had every reason to resent and dislike her. Worry and suspicion joined forces, making Tatiana fear what her presence meant.

"Blair Jones." Tatiana confirmed the woman's identity aloud. "You probably recognized her from her sexual harassment case against—"

"Marcus." Kimberly frowned, touching the edge of the phone lightly. "I had a crush on him when I was a teen. I got his autograph his rookie year when his team came to town to play the Mustangs. I never believed for a second he was guilty."

Tatiana wondered if she knew about her connection to Blair, but decided to leave well enough alone for now. She wanted to confront Blair before the ceremony and find out what the woman's intentions were. Her lawyer instincts told her she wasn't going to like the answer.

"You're not the only one," Tatiana remarked lightly, tucking her phone into her sequined yellow purse. "Would you excuse me while I go find Jean-Pierre before the wedding starts?"

Striding up the long aisle of carpet that had been rolled out on the sand, Tatiana did plan to seek out Jean-Pierre. She needed to warn him that Blair had somehow wrangled her way into the private family event. But first, she would try to find the woman herself, because every inch of her feminine intuition screamed that something was amiss. She didn't want her son—or her tentative relationship with Jean-Pierre—to be caught in the cross fire of whatever scandal was stirring around that woman.

"I've brought you a little something, boys." Leon Reynaud stood on the threshold of the Tides Ranch library that Gervais had opted to use as a gathering place for his groomsmen.

Jean-Pierre bounced a tennis ball on a huge piece of cypress wood fashioned into a desk at the back corner of the room. He'd been distracted with thoughts of Tatiana all morning, thinking about what Dempsey had said to him back in New Orleans.

So why is Gervais beating you to the altar?

It bothered Jean-Pierre that he hadn't managed to change that state of affairs. That he'd had a son born out of wedlock while Gervais was moving heaven and earth to ensure he put a ring on Erika's finger before his twins arrived. Now, with their vows just minutes away, he knew there would be no trip to any clerk's office with Tatiana before then. With that heavy weight of failure on his shoulders, he was only too glad to quit bouncing the tennis ball to see what Leon had to say.

"You're looking mighty sharp, Gramps," he called over his brothers' heads.

Dempsey and Gervais were taking turns remarking on how badly Henri's bow-tie-tying skills sucked, which was more a game of who could come up with better insults than anything, since Henri wore Tom Ford as well as anyone in the room. In matching silk tuxes, the Reynaud men cleaned up quite nicely.

"Same to you, son," Leon called, waving an impatient hand at the others to quiet them. "And the tie just needs a woman's touch, Henri," their grandfather muttered to the beleaguered Hurricanes starting quarterback. "If you got laid more, your tie would look just fine."

Gramps waggled shaggy white eyebrows and the four of them howled with laughter. Henri's laugh was loudest of all, since he tended to disappear in coat closets at the drop of a hat with his wife lately. He didn't seem to be suffering in that department.

But even better than Leon's perfectly timed insult was the fact that he looked so clear-eyed today. The old man was on his game despite the Alzheimer's and that pleased Jean-Pierre to no end. Their grandfather hadn't given them the most traditional upbringing once he'd stepped in to take charge with the unruly foursome, but he understood boys. He'd always been able to break the tension with a laugh. And despite his shortcomings, that showed a level of caring that would help Jean-Pierre be a better father.

When the room had quieted enough to hear him again, Leon set a wooden box on the desk beside Jean-Pierre. He opened it to reveal the dark Scotch whiskey inside.

"I'm not staying, you know. I've got a nursemaid hovering by the door even now, ready to box my ears if I enjoy the free bar at this shindig." He pointed a crooked finger at the archway where a placid, middle-aged woman checked her hair in a mirror. "But I wanted you all to enjoy a toast on me."

They crowded around the bottle—a sixty-two-year-old reserve blend—just as they had when Gramps brought a fifties-era Harley-Davidson bike to the ranch to give them a lesson in engine rebuilding. The motorcycle had been in crates when he bought the relic, but by the end of the summer they'd taken turns seeing how fast it would go on the private ranch roads.

No doubt it was the wedding making Jean-Pierre sentimental today as he thought about the past. And about how much he wished Tatiana would make things permanent between them so they could be a real family. Because even though that summer rebuilding the bike had been fun, he wanted a different kind of family for César.

"Thank you, *Grand-père*." Gervais clapped the older man on the shoulder. "I hope you'll stay for the toast even if you won't have a drink."

"No, I'm feeling my age and want to step out while I'm still fresh." He shook his head while Dempsey found glasses in a bar cabinet and Henri opened the bottle. "This is a day for the young. Enjoy it, boys. I'm proud of you all."

Jean-Pierre was heartbroken to see Leon's eyes mist over. But then their grandfather stalked out of the room toward his nurse, taking her arm like an old-time suitor on a first date.

Gervais wasted no time pouring the Scotch, the dark amber liquid fragrant in a room grown more somber.

"To Leon." Gervais lifted his glass.

They all nodded agreement, their glasses raised. But they had a family tradition of toasting around the horn, so they all added one.

"To the groom," Jean-Pierre offered.

"To fatherhood," Dempsey added, shooting a meaning-ful look at both Jean-Pierre and Gervais.

"To family," Henri added, bringing his glass in for the clink.

Jean-Pierre downed his fast, never having been a hard-core whiskey drinker. But this was smooth and rich, with-out the burn of a cheaper blend.

Outside the library, he could see the wedding guests fill-ing in the seats down by the beach. He hadn't seen Tatiana since early that morning and he wanted to find her soon to be sure he sat near her after his brief part in the ceremony.

He wondered if she'd been looking for him since he'd lost track of the passing hours in the library.

"Gentlemen?" The minister stepped into the room, a friend of Gervais's from Louisiana. "We'll need to take our places outside. It's time."

As they filed out, Dempsey hung back to walk with him.

"Today is the day. You know that, right?" Dempsey tugged his elbow to slow him down.

"It seems like a good evening for a sunset wedding," he agreed pleasantly.

"It's a good night for a proposal," Dempsey asserted with the authority of a lifetime matchmaker. Too bad he was just a nosy football coach who actually had no idea when the right time to propose might be.

"We'll see." Jean-Pierre had been thinking about it, in fact. There was a boathouse on the Tides Ranch that re-minded him of the one where he'd taken Tatiana to fool around back when they'd been dating.

That had significance, right? He wanted to show her he was trying. That he cared about how she felt and what she thought. Yet he also knew time was of the essence. He wanted to be married when they introduced César to the press and the longer they waited to the tie the knot, the greater the risk of discovery. And once the press knew about the baby, wouldn't she be less likely to say yes? As it stood now, Jean-Pierre suspected that she felt at least some social pressure to marry.

But once the news was out and she weathered that storm, what if she decided she didn't need to wed?

"You have a ring, right?" Dempsey asked.

"Since when are you the local ambassador of marriage?" He'd actually had a ring at the ready all week, but he wanted to find the right moment. As he exited the side stairs of the main ranch house, Jean-Pierre searched the wedding guests for a sign of Tatiana.

He'd seen the yellow gown she planned to wear hanging in a clear plastic garment bag, but had left before she'd dressed. When he'd seen her last, she'd been backed up against the white tile wall of the shower stall, her cheeks suffused with red from what they'd shared under the hot rush of water.

"I'm looking out for you, and you know it. You're rolling the dice with your reputation and hers, too. By not tackling this head-on, you're juicing up the press to get more and more inventive with headlines." His older brother straightened his tie as he hit the carpet. "Do you see Adelaide?"

Despite Dempsey's hard-edged veneer, he loved his former personal assistant with a passion he never bothered to disguise. He wasn't the kind to drag her into coat closets, but his eyes followed where she went.

"Dude." Jean-Pierre grabbed his brother's arm before he could leave. "How did you know it was the right time to ask Adelaide to marry you? That she'd say yes?"

"You think I knew she'd say yes?" Dempsey shook his head, as disappointed as if Jean-Pierre was a rookie who didn't understand a play. "Brother, you have to go all in even when you don't have any idea. Put yourself on the line. Or I promise you, she'll never say yes."

Without a single word of encouragement, his brother spun on his heel and melted into the crowd to find Adelaide, leaving Jean-Pierre just as clueless as before.

So it wasn't exactly ideal timing that Tatiana found him then, her dark curls spilling over one bare shoulder in a side-swept hairstyle that exposed the smooth skin of her neck. As always, she looked good enough to eat.

But he didn't have any idea how to tell her he wanted more from her than that. That he wanted to be a husband to her. A father to their son. He knew that without question.

"Blair Jones is here," she blurted suddenly, her words a hushed hiss of sound. Her expression, he realized, was venomous.

"Your client? The same Blair who lied about Marcus under oath?" He'd told her as much from the very beginning of the case, but Tatiana had explained to him—repeatedly—the rules of her job as Blair's attorney.

Now, however, she didn't appear as calmly accepting about Blair Jones as she had last winter.

"The same." Tatiana wrapped her hand around his forearm and turned him away from the crowd milling around the beach seating. A small chamber orchestra played, alternating zydeco music with classical selections from Erika's homeland. "And would you believe, she just admitted to me in private that she did exactly that? Lied under oath about Marcus?"

Jean-Pierre thought he might have spotted steam wafting up from her ears. Her cheeks were definitely red again, but not in the good way they'd been this morning in the shower. She was livid, he realized.

"I can't say I'm surprised," he admitted. "I thought as much all along."

Up front by the flower-covered archway, his brothers waved him over.

"Well, I'm reporting her to the judge," she growled, her eyes snapping emerald fire. The sea breeze lifted a few curls to blow them across her cheek. "I've been used by a greedy liar who doesn't care whose reputation she ruins." She bit her lip and arched up to speak more quietly close to his cheek. "But I'm also terrified she'll find out about César and run to the press for a lucrative payday."

Alarms blared in Jean-Pierre's head as he held up a finger to signal to his brothers that he'd be with them in a moment. After all the toasts about family, he didn't want to let them down today.

"Do you have any reason to believe she knows about our son?" They'd been so careful he didn't think that was possible. But then again, this woman—a menace to the football community for reasons he couldn't begin to guess—was now circulating among their closest friends and family.

Who knew what she might hear this weekend?

"No." Tatiana shook her head, biting her lip, rubbing her arms in a nervous shiver. "But I'm scared. And I have a bad feeling about her. I'm sure she was unhappy with me when I told her I was going to report her for perjury. Attorney-client privilege doesn't apply in this instance since I am no longer her lawyer and I wasn't acting as her lawyer when she spoke to me."

"You told her that?" His insides sank with foreboding.

"I was angry." Her eyes glistened. "I unknowingly helped her ruin an innocent man's reputation."

Jean-Pierre hauled her into a hug as the chamber orchestra finished their song. There were no words to make this better. The guilt in her eyes spoke volumes. It hadn't been her fault she'd believed her client and done her job. He saw that now and wished he could have been more levelheaded then. He held her tighter, pressing a kiss to her temple.

"The wedding is about to begin." He kissed her cheek. "We'll figure it out. Save me a seat and we'll talk afterward."

He didn't like walking away from her when she was so upset. But he had a duty to perform.

His sixth sense niggled in the back of his mind even as he reached the floral archway to wait with Gervais for his bride. Already he knew it was going to be a bad day for a marriage proposal of his own. He just hoped his proposal was the only thing ruined on a day that should be the happiest of his brother's life.

Twelve

The wedding reception was truly magical.

After the sunset beachside vows, guests were ushered into a hacienda pavilion built in the style of traditional Spanish colonial architecture. The tile floors and sun-bleached stone walls supported high arches looking out over the water. A dark tile roof protected them from the sun, while the ever-present solar panels collected the energy to keep the generators running. The chamber musicians had given up their spot to a popular country band and already the foreign princesses were dancing with dashing husbands in various hues of military dress and ornamentation. A few of the younger football players joined them, two-stepping circles around the more formal waltzes of their royal counterparts.

Greenery bedecked every archway and long ropes of ivy decorated the exposed beams overhead. The effect was like having a party in a secret garden. Erika had told Ta-

tiana earlier that they'd purchased the flowers and greens
back when they hoped to have the event on Lake Pontchartrain, but if the princess minded exchanging her vows on
a beach and having her reception in a hacienda instead,
no one would have ever guessed. She danced with Gervais long before any formal introduction of the couple,
and Tatiana couldn't help but admire a bride who didn't
stand on ceremony.

If a woman only had one wedding in her life, she deserved to have fun during every moment of it. That was
one of many reasons Tatiana was on the lookout for her
former client while Jean-Pierre consulted with Henri and
Dempsey in a far corner of the pavilion. She didn't want
more scandal to dim Erika's enjoyment of her day.

"I recognize this young woman all grown up." The
male voice close to Tatiana's elbow surprised her. "Care
to dance?"

She turned to find Leon Reynaud, the man who had
fired her father. Leon had been formidable well into his
seventies, but his age had caught up to him a bit. His shoulders had thinned and he'd lost some of the impressive
height that had been a genetic gift to his football-playing
grandsons. Wispy white hair and overgrown white eyebrows didn't detract from the elegance of his appearance,
however. She took in the crisp black tuxedo and starched
French cuffs turned back from gnarled fingers as he offered his arm.

"I'd love to, sir, but I'm waiting to speak to your grandson. And are you sure you remember me?" She would be
surprised if he knew her. He'd never paid her much attention when she'd visited their home in the past since he'd
usually been closeted with her father in business meetings
the whole time.

"You're the daughter of the infamous Jack Doucet, if I

don't miss my guess. I fired him." He said it with a jovial air, loud enough to turn heads of people nearby. Perhaps he didn't realize how devastating it had been for her father and her whole family at the time—and for years afterward.

They didn't have the resources that the Reynauds did, and losing a lucrative job over a petty grievance between friends had shaken the Doucet family to its foundation.

This week, especially, she'd found herself wondering what might have become of her relationship with Jean-Pierre if they hadn't been separated so acrimoniously back then.

"You have a good memory." She had changed a lot since she was seventeen. Especially in the last few months. Plus, she'd thought the older man suffered from Alzheimer's.

"You should tell my nurse," he grumbled, pointing toward a middle-aged woman in a pressed gray uniform standing a few feet away and taking photos of the table arrangements. "She doesn't think I can remember anything."

"Your nurse?" She studied the woman more closely and realized now the older man was confused after all. "That can't be her. I recognize that woman from Gervais's house. She's on the housekeeping staff."

Leon's eyes bulged. "Confound it, woman!" He turned on the housekeeper and gripped her arm. "I knew you weren't my health-care worker."

His raised voice attracted more turned heads even though the band continued to play. Jean-Pierre was by Tatiana's side almost instantly, while Henri and Dempsey attempted to take their grandfather aside.

"What's wrong?" Jean-Pierre asked, slipping an arm around her shoulders, the muscles hard and firm against her.

She pointed to the maid who darted out of the pavilion the moment Leon released his hold.

"That woman." Tatiana pointed her out, a sinking feeling in her gut. "Leon thought it was his caregiver, but I know she was the same woman who greeted us the night we had dinner at your brother's home. I just said I didn't think that could be his nurse and—"

"Who in the hell was she?" Leon was shouting now, loud enough to pull Gervais away from his new bride.

"Gramps, what's wrong?" He tried, like his brothers, to usher the agitated man aside, but the more they tried to move him, the more belligerent he became.

"You all sent me to a strange place with a woman I didn't even know and tried to convince me she was my nurse." Leon scoffed as if the word left a bad taste. "She's a harlot and a liar. She told me I missed seeing Jean-Pierre's son, but I know damn well Jean-Pierre isn't a father yet."

Tatiana froze.

Everyone close to her seemed to turn stone-still as well. Jean-Pierre looked to her helplessly while his brothers looked at him, all of them waiting for someone to say something. To announce whatever story it was that they wanted to use.

Now was the time, while a whole pavilion full of wedding guests listened. Including Blair Jones, who would surely have reason to want to spread the gossip with malicious glee after Tatiana had threatened to turn her in for perjury.

Tatiana shook her head at Jean-Pierre. She had no idea what to say. If she'd had a good cover story for César, she would have given it out months ago instead of running off to the Caribbean to give birth privately.

"Come on, Gramps." Dempsey slung an arm around his grandfather as some of the fight seemed to slip out of Leon. "Let's step away to figure out what's going on and let Gervais have his wedding, okay?"

"Sure," Leon said agreeably, although his expression remained troubled. "You're a good boy, Theo. Always were my favorite."

Tatiana's heart squeezed painfully in her chest as she listened to him say words destined to hurt his other children—and knowing she'd also lost her window to admit the truth. That she and Jean-Pierre had a child together. End of story.

Wasn't it? But if so, why had they waited so long to reveal it, missed so many opportunities and flirted with disaster this way? It was as if they'd set themselves up for failure.

She looked at Jean-Pierre, the man who'd come back into her life to help her discover the truth about her lying client. She hadn't listened to him then, and their argument had turned into something beautiful and complicated. A night she would never regret.

But these last days, she'd hoped they were moving toward that common ground they'd shared long ago when they were teenagers. He'd taken her to his bed with all the passion she'd once dreamed of and more. But he still hadn't claimed to love her. And she knew him well enough to know he'd never speak those words if he didn't mean them. She could hardly believe he'd simply overlooked them…

"Tatiana." He hooked his arm around her now, guiding her from the pavilion and out into the clear, warm night. He purposely walked her past Kimberly and stopped, interrupting the woman's phone call. "Kimberly, I'd owe you a favor forever if you would cut the power to that cell tower as fast as possible."

"Seriously?" She frowned.

"We've got leaks all over the place and I want to sit on a story to let the bride and groom have their day." His hand gripped Tatiana's waist gently, his fingers grazing her hip.

"I do love being off the grid." Kimberly grinned, stabbing a few buttons on her phone. "And I don't mind going incognito for however long you like. Although, I've got to warn you, if my father finds out we're disconnected, he'll be on the first boat out here."

"I just need to buy some time," Jean-Pierre assured her while the country band turned up their amps and the fiddle player kicked into high gear.

"Done." She flipped her phone toward him so he could see. "Look close because I'll lose the image as soon as I shut down that tower." She showed him a picture of a cell tower disguised as a pine tree on the screen, then hit a button.

The image vanished. Thanking her, he continued toward a section of the island Tatiana hadn't seen before. It wasn't the dock where their ferry had parked, but it was a pier of some sort. And, she could see by the moonlight, a boathouse.

"Where are we going?" She had worn low heels for the wedding, but there'd been carpet on the beach. Now, she tugged the shoes off and left them on a planter incorporated into the landscaping.

"I thought about taking you to the boathouse on Lake Pontchartrain. But there wasn't enough time, so this is going to have to do." He slid off his shoes, too, and left them by hers.

"We used to fool around in the boathouse." She'd fallen in love with him there.

Of course, that was a long time ago and she'd buried all those feelings. Did he know they were breaking through all the barriers she'd put around them? That the past and present had mingled in her mind and heart, helping her to see the old hints of the boy she'd loved along with the more reserved man she'd carefully avoided ever since he'd come to New York two years ago to play for the Gladiators?

"It remains my fondest teenage memory." He held her hand as they walked out onto the pier and then up the steps of a simple boathouse with a deck on the flat roof.

Jean-Pierre led her past a small shed containing extra lifesaving gear and utilitarian jackets to the front railing that looked out over the gulf.

She wanted to ask him more about that. To hear why he remembered those days fondly, too. She'd always suspected his heart hardened toward her when she'd told him to leave and not come back—a directive given by her father, but one that she meant since his family had hurt hers irreparably.

Only by being the best in her class had they afforded Columbia. Only by being the best in her job had she afforded her apartment, and even then, she'd been fortunate to have a connection in the law firm who knew the building owner. But she didn't want to win cases at the expense of the truth. She never would have taken that case if she'd known that Blair Jones lied through her teeth.

"Who do you think that woman was who posed as Leon's nurse?" She felt as if she had too many puzzle pieces that she couldn't fit together. And maybe she was avoiding thinking about what mattered most. One benefit of having the truth come out about César would be she didn't have to hide him any longer. She wasn't going to live for the sake of keeping up appearances anymore.

"Someone looking for a payout by obtaining unauthorized pictures of the event." Jean-Pierre shrugged. "You said she was taking photographs, so I assume she planned to sell out the family and offer wedding photos to the highest tabloid bidder."

"But doesn't Leon have a real caregiver? Do you think the nurse made the trip?" She felt worried about him after seeing the way he'd veered from clarity to confusion and back again. It must be frightening to lose your grip on your memories.

"We'll find out," Jean-Pierre promised her, taking her hands in both of his. "She might have made a deal to split the payday with the nurse, or just paid the woman outright. It's very difficult to find loyal employees, especially when scandal draws us into the headlines and the price for a story goes sky-high. Once interest in us dies down, the staff will go back to honoring those confidentiality agreements they all signed."

"It's my fault that interest really ramped up right before the wedding. I'm so sorry. I never meant for any of this to spill over into Gervais and Erika's special day."

"Erika is tough. She would probably be the first to say it's not a royal wedding without a tabloid crasher." Jean-Pierre tried to smile, but she could tell the turn of events troubled him, too.

"What should we do next?" She shivered as the breeze turned cooler.

A wave splashed against the boathouse with a little extra force, enough to cause a fine spray of mist on her skin.

"I hope we will do what I've wanted all along." He withdrew a ring box from the breast pocket of his tuxedo jacket.

Her heart stilled. Her mouth went dry.

Jean-Pierre, the father of her child, got down on one knee in the moonlight. She could hardly process what was happening. She'd expected a game plan. A strategy for coming up with a story. Not a heartfelt proposal.

Hope stirred within. Maybe their time together had cracked open his heart and made him realize he loved her after all.

That their common ground could be so much more beautiful than just co-parenting according to a contract.

"Tatiana." He looked up at her, his eyes as dark as the

water below, his expression inscrutable. "You and César are more important to me than anything in the world."

In her old fantasies of this moment—the ones she'd dreamed up a decade ago—he'd led his speech with "I love you and I can't live without you." But she recognized that she wasn't speaking to her eighteen-year-old boyfriend, dammit. Jean-Pierre was a formidable man. A world-renowned athlete. A business tycoon with interests all over the globe.

For him to say she was the most important thing in his world—along with their baby—was saying a great deal.

"When I look at you holding our son in your arms, I want to give you the world. To make sure that nothing ever hurts you. To keep you safe forever." He kissed the back of her left hand and then the left ring finger. "Nothing would bring me more happiness than if you would be my wife."

Her heart pounded so loudly she wondered if she'd missed that he also wanted to give her his heart. But maybe he included that when he said he'd give her the world? Worry made her heart beat crazily as he opened up the ring box and withdrew a magnificent diamond, a huge, sparkling pear-shaped central stone with two smaller stones to either side. There was an elegant simplicity about it, but her longstanding interest in appearances told her that it was at least eight carats. If she was still a woman who cared about those things, that ring would have dazzled her.

It still dazzled her.

But had she missed hearing the one thing her heart most craved?

She swallowed hard.

"Jean-Pierre." She savored his name on her lips. How many times had she stenciled it on notebooks or in her diary once upon a time, adding his last name to her first? "You know how nervous I can get. And I hope to remember this moment always." After all they'd shared the last few days, after the way he'd made love to her, surely that had nudged his heart into a more tender place toward her? "Do you…love me?"

It had cost her so much to ask. And she had her answer instantly. It was there, in the fleeting panic in his dark eyes.

The hesitation that told her this was the last question he wanted to field during a proposal of marriage.

"Never mind." She rushed to fill that moment of silence, thrusting his ring back in his palm. "I'm being overly sentimental, I know. You didn't expect that from me with all my lawyerly practicality, did you?" She shook her head, babbling and unable to stop herself since her eyes burned and she couldn't bear for him to see her cry. Damn these postpartum hormones still having their way with her. "And so foolish of me, too, since you had no problem walking away from me after we were together last winter. I mean, who walks away if they have an ounce of tenderness in their hearts?"

"Please, listen." He was on his feet, tucking the ring box in his pocket again.

"No. I don't think I will." She held up her hands defensively. "I don't think I can. I was listening very hard a moment ago, and when I didn't hear what I hoped to, I had to ask about it, embarrassing us both." She headed for the stairs, needing to put space between them. "Now, I'm going to return to my room and we can figure out how to co-parent when I'm not completely mortified over needing footnotes to explain my marriage proposals."

He chased her down, capturing her before she could descend the wooden steps.

"You're the only woman to ever break my heart, Tatiana. The. Only." His face was inches from hers, his grip unshakable. "I put everything on the line to come to New

York at eighteen and see you. To tell you all the things I have a hard time saying now. Leon made sure my life was hell afterward since I left without his knowledge or permission and he was furious that I would dare to step foot in Jack Doucet's house. But none of that mattered to me because you wouldn't even speak to me."

She spun to face him, her yellow dress swishing around her legs. "I was just seventeen years old, for heaven's sake. My father made me say that."

He thrust his fingers through his hair in exasperation. "I realize that now. Do you think it mattered to me then?" He set her aside gently and shook his head, as if the memory was something he didn't want to think about. "I became a much different person after that, and I know you did, too. It was no fault of yours or mine. But you, of all people, should understand that I don't think I can fall in love in a week these days. I turned off that switch a long time ago."

"You've never been in love? Ever." She didn't believe him. "If you've never been in love, then how do you know what a broken heart is?"

"I'm twenty-eight years old, and call it a cop-out—but I'm married to the game."

"You can't be serious." It added insult to injury that he would use that for an excuse not to get close to someone.

His fierce expression never wavered. "It takes all my time. All my brainpower. Every ounce of my physical energy. Normally, I'm training for hours every day. This week I've sacrificed workout after workout trying to show you how much I want to be a part of César's life. And yours. I wish that was good enough for you, because I'm offering you more than I've ever wanted to share with anyone else."

"So I should be thrilled that I rate higher than your free weights this week?" She wanted to throttle him. To make him see how ridiculous that sounded. To make him stop breaking *her* heart.

"I hoped you would be happy to sleep in my arms at night and give us more time to fall in love." The sincerity in his eyes hit home, finding a place in her heart.

Why hadn't he said this before? Or did he only go to this argument as his plan B? She didn't want to be his checkdown because he couldn't complete the long pass. She wouldn't be his safe option.

"Marriage is forever for me. I won't gamble on a maybe." She knew he'd said all he could say. That he'd dug as deep as he could for her.

But no matter how much she wanted it to be enough, she knew she would always feel as if she'd settled. As if she'd been too concerned about appearances and married the father of her son to quiet any gossip.

"I respect that." He shook his head, his proud shoulders falling just a little. "But I'm not going to lie. It hurts like hell to think I won't be with you and César every day."

She couldn't agree more on the hurt-like-hell part. But they'd reached an impasse. And no matter how valiantly Jean-Pierre fought to keep a lid on the news of their son's existence, the story was going to come out all too soon.

And despite what she'd hoped, there wouldn't be any wedding news attached to it. Unable to return to someone else's happy event, she descended the boathouse stairs and headed toward the main house, knowing all that remained for her here was to pack her bags.

Thirteen

Good game, Reynaud, Jean-Pierre thought to himself—heavy on the sarcasm—as yet another poorly thrown pass got picked off in practice the week after Gervais's wedding.

Back in New York at the Gladiators' training facility, Jean-Pierre finished up his last practice before the game against the Hurricanes two days from now. The team would fly to New Orleans in the morning and have a meal together the night before the brother-against-brother matchup the media had been hyping for weeks.

His ill-fated reunion with the coach's daughter had only revved the hype to a fever pitch, putting the game in the public eye in a way that went far beyond the interest of football fans. Since news of their son had hit the papers the day after Gervais's wedding, the press had mobbed the Gladiators' practice field during the sanctioned media times, making it impossible to duck their questions. While Jack Doucet—who'd barely spoken to him this week, preferring to glare darkly at him—had texted him a reminder that he did not need to discuss his personal life in the interviews, the questions were nonstop.

Will you live in the same state as your son? What are Tatiana's plans now? As if he flipping knew. As if she cared about him enough to tell him. Her law firm had sent him an efficient packet of options for possible co-parenting agreements, but he'd been too disheartened to wade through the legalese.

"Get your head in the game!" the quarterback coach shouted at him across the field as if Jean-Pierre was a distracted JV player and not one of the league's elite.

Actually, with how he'd been playing all week in practice, the JV comparison felt kind of accurate.

The coach's whistle trilled from the sidelines, calling an end to the day's team workout. Jean-Pierre would still prepare for hours with the offensive coordinator, with the quarterback coach and then on his own to be sure he understood the game plan and his opponent. But whereas at another time he might enjoy the challenge of going up against Henri and really pitting their strengths against each other, this week he felt as though someone had put a fist in his chest and stolen his heart. No doubt this was what heartbreak felt like.

The ache was so literal it was ridiculous.

And how ass-backward was it of him to realize what all that hurt was about now that it was killing him. He loved Tatiana. He was just too blind to recognize that feeling for what it was. He'd spent so much time living in his head, methodically moving through his life, that he'd forgotten how messy and painful emotions could be. You couldn't control them the way you could manage a game plan or manipulate a play.

"Reynaud!" The shout didn't surprise him. Someone

or another had been chewing his ass all week for his piss-poor efforts on the field.

Turning, he was surprised to see Jack Doucet himself storming toward him. He noticed most of the rest of the team had already headed indoors to shower up and head home. Actually, now that he thought about it, some of them would be talking to the press since there was a scheduled media hour after this practice.

More time to face the firing squad about his shortcomings as a man. He hadn't even managed to communicate how much he loved the mother of his firstborn. Thinking about that made him welcome whatever diatribe Jack Doucet had in store for him.

"Yes, sir?" Jean Pierre lifted a towel from the metal bench along the sidelines, swiping the sweat from his face and hair. The team had practiced outdoors in the November cold, but the sharp gray wind didn't penetrate a helmet.

"What the hell do you think you're doing, boy?" The coach slammed his clipboard onto the bench with enough force to make the metal ring. "You've got the eyes of the whole football nation on you, and you're lumbering through this week like a homesick rookie."

A kind assessment, in Jean-Pierre's opinion. He nodded, knowing the coach wasn't close to finished.

"As your coach, I'm so furious with you I want to start your backup." He pointed a finger in his face. "But as the grandfather of your son, I'm going to ignore all that for the sake of my daughter and ask you what you're going to do to fix this mess you made with her?"

Surprised at the question, which bordered on warm and fuzzy from a coach with a legendary temper, Jean-Pierre lifted a wary gaze to Tatiana's father. The older man glared at him, but there were lines on his brow that suggested he was worried more than he was angry. Concern etched his features.

With nothing left to lose, Jean-Pierre told him the truth.

"She needed me to tell her I loved her. And I, like the cerebral half-ass that I am, hadn't worked all that out in my head yet." Remembering the look in her eyes gutted him. "In other words, when the game was on the line, I choked."

"Who looks for love in their head?" The coach's face screwed up as though he'd gulped down grapefruit juice. "You figure that out in your heart, Reynaud."

"Not my area of expertise, sir." He looped the sweaty towel around his neck and scooped up his helmet to head indoors.

The coach held up a hand to stop him. "You didn't answer my question. How are you going to fix this?"

The pain in Jean-Pierre's chest tightened into a knot.

"I proposed twice." He'd put a lot of thought and effort into the second go-round, thinking about what he'd say and studying diamond choices. Hell, he'd even taken her to a boathouse roof, a nod to their past he was sure she would appreciate. But he'd been focusing on the peripherals and not the only thing that mattered to her. "Your daughter isn't a woman to give unlimited chances."

Jack Doucet shook his head. "My daughter is a woman who deserves to know she's worthy of love. So even if she sends your ass to the showers for a third time, I suggest you inform her about what's in here." He jabbed his finger into Jean-Pierre's chest protector with enough force to send him back a step.

Before he could answer, the coach turned on his heel and barreled away. He was only a few yards away when he called over his shoulder.

"And get your head in the damn game while you're at it."

Easier said than done.

Dropping to the bench on the sidelines, he reached into his bag, where he'd stashed his water bottle and head-phones. Finding his phone, he gritted his teeth and pulled up Tatiana's contact information. Her image filled his screen for a moment, her dark curls and pretty smile so beautiful that he couldn't breathe.

Maybe the people who are slow to love are the ones who love the most, he texted fast, knowing he needed to say it before he second-guessed himself. *By the time they've finished studying all the angles and assessing the situation, they are heart-deep. Please see me after the game on Sunday.*

He wasn't surprised when there was no reply.

But he would honor his coach's suggestion because it was a good one. Tatiana deserved to know how he felt, even if she'd already closed her heart to him forever.

Tatiana caused a stir in the Zephyr Dome when she arrived at the Hurricanes' home field in New Orleans on Sunday. The tabloid coverage of her romance with Jean-Pierre had spilled into the mainstream media so that she'd become a recognizable face in this particular crowd. Although she'd had a security guard escort her to her seat—a measure taken by a stadium staffer who'd quickly realized she was starting a mob scene in the concession area—Tatiana had been approached by one fan after another before the game. She'd obtained box seats in the first row closest to the field, so they were excellent seats. But seeing the at-tention she received, an usher had requested that she move to the Hurricane owner's private box—an invitation she knew was a sought-after commodity even among celeb-rities. Yet she felt too awkward to sit with Jean-Pierre's family after the way she'd left the Tides Ranch during Erika's wedding.

She was only here because Jean-Pierre had sent her a text asking to see her.

Pulling her phone from her purse shortly before half-time, she double-checked the message that had landed in her in-box on Friday.

Maybe the people who are slow to love are the ones who love the most. By the time they've finished studying all the angles and assessing the situation, they are heart-deep. Please see me after the game on Sunday.

She'd reread the words so many times she could have recited them in her sleep. She probably *had* the last two nights, in fact. But seeing them on the screen of her phone, with Jean-Pierre's name at the top, reminded her that he had been the author of those cryptic lines.

Not that she'd come to the game with any illusions about his feelings. But he'd asked to see her. And since he had yet to return any of the paperwork outlining their custody arrangement for César, she thought seeing him would facilitate that necessary step. It was all very logical and practical, just like him.

Except how did he know that those who were slow to love might love in any special way? The question had replayed over and over in her thoughts ever since the text had arrived.

Now, as the whistle blew signaling the end of the first half of the game, the teams on the field relaxed and strode toward their respective sidelines before heading into the locker room. The music in the stadium increased in volume and many fans stood to seek refreshments in the concession area or wait in long lines at the bathrooms. Tatiana stayed in her seat, wondering if she was crazy for being here. She'd convinced her mother to fly down and babysit

César for her during the game. It had been hard watching Henri and Jean-Pierre face off, but they were tied going into the half.

Fourteen to fourteen.

"Look, Ms. Doucet!" A fan wearing black and gold Hurricanes' colors and team gear on every part of her body turned in her seat next to her and gripped Tatiana's knee. "You're on the big screen!"

Following where the woman pointed with her eyes, Tatiana spied an image of herself on the jumbo board over the football field. She tried to smile since the fans were cheering for her even though she'd worn a Gladiators jersey, but she saw that her pretend smile looked more like a grimace.

As the electronic screen switched over to highlights from the game, the fans cheered for other things and Tatiana allowed her attention to return to the field. The players vacated the sidelines and the cheerleaders took up positions. Automatically, her gaze sought out Jean-Pierre, only to see him still on the sidelines, scanning the bleachers.

He shielded his eyes from the sun since the retractable dome was open today. Close to where he stood, fans pointed him downfield.

In her direction.

Heart in her throat, she watched the highly unorthodox interaction. Her father would be furious if his quarterback didn't get into the locker room pronto. The team made adjustments during halftime and Jean-Pierre would have a key role to play. Except now the fans were all in an uproar because he was jogging alongside the high wall of the bleachers.

Toward her.

"Tatiana!" he shouted, lifting a hand to give a wave. Helmet removed, he was sweaty and his face had a smudge on one cheek, as if someone's cleat had landed on his face. But his dark eyes were locked on her; he was oblivious to the fans, who were going berserk to have him this close. It didn't matter that he played for the opposing side. He was a Reynaud. One of the game's elite.

And he only had eyes for her.

Standing, she leaned over the rail, not even caring that all the eyes of section A-101 were following their every movement.

"Hi," she said, perplexed. It wasn't like Jean-Pierre to pull unorthodox moves. That had always been Henri's claim to fame. "What are you doing?"

He leaped up to grip the metal railing in front of her and the fans shouted and crowded her. She hadn't realized half of section A-101 had left their seats to get closer to the action. Jean-Pierre hoisted himself higher and fans reached over as if to pull him into the stands.

She feared a riot or a stampede, but Jean-Pierre just shook off the help with a grin that she recognized as his public face, the disarming charm that all the Reynauds employed with ease when they needed it.

"I've got this!" he called to the fans. "Just here to see this beautiful lady."

Female fans swooned. She could honestly hear the collective sigh.

"Jean-Pierre?" She wondered if this was a publicity stunt, but that would be so out of character for him. "What's going on?"

"I love you." His muscles flexed as he held himself there like a gymnast on the high bar. "I needed to tell you in person, not in a text. But I couldn't wait another minute."

She'd fallen off the swings once as a girl and it had felt just like this. Like the wind was knocked out of her. Like she couldn't figure out quite what had happened.

"I don't understand."

"Your father will be losing his mind in the locker room any minute." Jean-Pierre glanced down the sidelines at the runway that led into the visiting team's locker room. "I have to go. But don't leave afterward, okay? I want to tell you better than this. I just…" He shook his head. "Damn, Tatiana. I don't expect anything from you. I just want you to listen."

Before she could reply, he kissed her hard on the cheek and then dropped out of sight. As he hit the ground with a thud, the crowd went wild.

The whole, entire stadium.

Because the jumbo screen was trained on Jean-Pierre even now, following the sideline antics with an up close view for everyone to see.

As he jogged toward the runway, helmet in hand, she wondered if he knew he'd just declared his love for her in front of the whole world. Then, remembering this was Jean-Pierre, the most methodical, analytical, cautious QB in the game of football, she realized of course he knew what he'd done. He'd given her a moment that was unexpected, unscripted and from the heart.

She couldn't have asked for more proof that he'd handed her his whole heart.

The total stranger in the Hurricanes gear next to her opened her arms to her, sharing a phenomenal game moment in the way fans do. It was crazy. And yet, she allowed herself to be hugged, congratulated and feted by all of section A-101, who were beside themselves with being part of a famous love story.

When they'd finally freed her shortly before the second half started, she allowed the usher to escort her out of the box and up the stairs. She definitely needed to talk to Jean-Pierre for real. Without an audience.

But now, she had every reason in the world to hope this really was the start of a famous love story. The emphasis, at last, on *love*.

Waiting in the wives' lounge on the same corridor as the visiting team's locker room, Tatiana could watch game highlights from the brother-versus-brother showdown. The Gladiators had lost even though Jean-Pierre had set a new career high for pass yardage. He'd played an incredible game, but the Gladiators came up short after Henri marched his team down the field with forty-five seconds left to put them in field-goal range, beating his brother by three points.

The game had been epic, to steal an overblown adjective from the excited sportscasters whose coverage she now watched. Almost epic enough to overshadow Jean-Pierre's halftime declaration of love, but not quite. She'd seen footage of his leap up to the stands at least five times while she waited for him to emerge. Only a handful of other women waited with her since the press interviews were still going on. Contractually, the players had to stay for a certain amount of time afterward to field questions.

Unless they were injured.

And in one of the kindest things her father had ever done for her, he texted her after the game to let her know that Jean-Pierre was being seen by a team doctor for a possible concussion. She'd been around the game—and her wily dad—long enough to interpret the text as his shorthand for saying that he'd officially excused his quarterback from press interviews. In other words, the coach had sprung his star early for her sake by supplying the media with the only legitimate excuse for not attending.

When the door opened and Jean-Pierre's large frame filled it, his dark hair still damp from his shower and his attire a standard issue team T-shirt, he didn't look like the bayou billionaire who'd escorted her to his brother's wedding last week or introduced her to foreign royalty. He looked like her high school boyfriend after a rough practice, a bit banged up and bruised with a scrape over one eye. But his eyes definitely lit up at the sight of her.

"You're here. I hoped you would be, but I wasn't sure." Shouldering a duffel bag, he gestured toward the exit on the other side of the lounge. "Do you mind if we find someplace else to talk?"

"Sure." She hugged her arms around herself, feeling as nervous as a girl waiting to be asked to the prom—even though she was pretty sure the boy she liked now liked her back. "How long before you have to be ready for the team flight back to New York?"

"It leaves at seven." He held the door for her that led out into a quiet hallway. "But the coach knows I might need further evaluation from a local doctor, so I'm able to fly back tomorrow if necessary."

She couldn't quite smother a laugh. "My father must really want us to have time to talk."

"He made that very clear." He strode toward a side exit and nodded at the door. "My brothers sent a limo for me. It's in the home team lot. If you want we could sit in there."

"Okay. My mother has César, so I don't need to worry about him." As she followed Jean-Pierre through the maze of corridors beneath the Zephyr Dome, she was glad to be with someone who knew the lay of the land. She was just glad to be near Jean-Pierre, period. She couldn't wait to sit beside him and look in his eyes. Find out what on earth was going through that mind of his. "I hope Dad didn't pressure you to—"

"Absolutely not." He steered her toward a limo nearby.

"He floored me, actually, by giving me the best advice of my life."

"My father?" She hurried to keep pace with his long strides.

A driver exited the limo and took Jean-Pierre's bag before tipping his cap at Tatiana. While the chauffer stored the item, Jean Pierre opened the back door to the vehicle. They got in and he locked it from inside. Then he used a remote to lock the privacy window.

White roses filled a vase beside a bottle of champagne in an ice bucket. The black leather bench seats let them sit close to one another while, up front, the driver fired the engine to life. She had no idea where they were going and she didn't care. All her attention was focused on the man beside her.

"Your dad surprised me. He didn't say anything when I first got back to New York, but by Friday, he stormed over and demanded to know what was going on between us since I'd been screwing up every way possible in practice."

"I didn't tell my parents anything when I got back. I was too upset to talk about it and they respected that." Her eyes scanned his face and it was all she could do not to lift her fingers to the scrape above his eyebrow. But she wanted to hear more, to find out what had gone on with him since she left the Tides Ranch.

"I was very blunt when I told him how I'd messed up with you. How I hadn't recognized what I was feeling because I was so busy thinking it all through."

"You do like to analyze things." She remembered his mathematically drawn wine labels, his lettering perfectly spaced.

"Right. And he said you don't find love in your head. You find it in your heart."

That did not compute for Tatiana. "I can't imagine my father saying anything like that."

"Picture the words infused with more cursing while he yells them at me."

She fell against Jean-Pierre as the limo took a hard turn exiting the parking garage. The feel of his muscular body against hers made her want to curl up and stay there. With an effort, she straightened and met his gaze evenly.

"That I can envision." She refused to ask him again about love. She'd been mortified enough for one lifetime on that score.

"But by then I already knew the truth. That I love you like crazy. I could tell because when you left the ranch it was like you'd ripped my heart out and took it with you."

She'd felt that way, too. As if she'd left her heart on the island with him. Still, she waited.

He took her shoulders in his hands and squared her to face him on the seat.

"I am in pain without you. I love you and I'm sure of it. This love will never go away." He stroked the outside of her arms, sliding his fingers along the silky sleeves of the Gladiators jersey she'd worn to the game. "I understand if you don't trust me enough to take another chance with me. But your father was right when he told me that you deserved to know how I feel."

If the "I love you" part hadn't hit her heart like an arrow, straight and true, then the last part would have sealed the deal. He didn't expect anything from her in return. He just wanted her to know.

Tears sprang to her eyes and her throat closed up with too many emotions to name.

"I love you, too." Her words were a harsh whisper, the only sound she could make over the burn in her throat. "So much."

He folded her in his strong arms and she leaned into him. Home at last.

He held her tight, with a fierceness that told her how much he'd missed her. How much he'd hurt without her. She understood this reserved man so much better than she'd given herself credit for. She'd fallen in love with him a long time ago, and no matter what he said about being a different man now, she saw her old love inside the new one.

"Let's not be apart anymore." She levered back to look up at him, realizing they'd left the stadium and were on the highway that led west toward Lake Pontchartrain.

"I'd give anything to take you home with me." He stroked a thumb along her cheek and tipped her face up to his. "Forever."

When his kiss brushed her lips, she twined her arms around his neck and he pulled her into his lap. Tomorrow was soon enough to get married. For tonight, no matter the scandal, she was going to go home with Jean-Pierre Reynaud, the man who'd always had her heart.

* * * * *

If you loved this novel,
don't miss any of the stories in the
BAYOU BILLIONAIRES *series*
from **USA TODAY** *bestselling author Catherine Mann*
and
Joanne Rock

HIS PREGNANT PRINCESS BRIDE
by Catherine Mann

HIS SECRETARY'S SURPRISE FIANCÉ
by Joanne Rock

REUNITED WITH THE REBEL BILLIONAIRE
by Catherine Mann

If you're on Twitter, tell us what you think of
Harlequin Desire! #harlequindesire

COMING NEXT MONTH FROM

Available June 7, 2016

#2449 REDEEMING THE BILLIONAIRE SEAL
Billionaires and Babies • by Lauren Canan
Navy SEAL Chance Masters is only back on the family ranch until his next deployment, but can the all-grown-up girl next door struggling to raise her infant niece convince him his rightful place is at home?

#2450 A BRIDE FOR THE BOSS
Texas Cattleman's Club: Lies and Lullabies
by Maureen Child
When Mac's overworked assistant quits, he's left floundering. But when she challenges the wealthy rancher to spend two weeks not working—with *her*—he soon realizes all the pleasures he's been missing...

#2451 A PREGNANCY SCANDAL
Love and Lipstick • by Kat Cantrell
One broken rule. One night of passion. Now...one accidental pregnancy! A marriage of convenience is the only way to prevent a scandal for the popular senator and his no-frills CFO lover—until their union becomes so much more...

#2452 THE BOSS AND HIS COWGIRL
Red Dirt Royalty • by Silver James
Clay Barron is an oil magnate bred for great things. Nothing can stop his ambition—except the beautiful assistant from his hometown. Will his craving for the former cowgirl mean a choice between love and success?

#2453 ARRANGED MARRIAGE, BEDROOM SECRETS
Courtesan Brides • by Yvonne Lindsay
To prepare for his arranged marriage, Prince Thierry hires a mysterious beauty to tutor him in romance. His betrothed, Mila, mischievously takes the woman's place. But as the prince falls for his "forbidden" lover, Mila's revelations will threaten all they hold dear...

#2454 TRAPPED WITH THE MAVERICK MILLIONAIRE
From Mavericks to Married • by Joss Wood
Years ago, one kiss from a hockey superstar rocked Rory's world. Now Mac needs her—as his live-in physical therapist! Despite their explosive chemistry, she keeps her hands off—until one hot island night as a storm rages...

REQUEST YOUR FREE BOOKS!
2 FREE NOVELS PLUS 2 FREE GIFTS!

H HARLEQUIN®

Desire

ALWAYS POWERFUL, PASSIONATE AND PROVOCATIVE

YES! Please send me 2 FREE Harlequin® Desire novels and my 2 FREE gifts (gifts are worth about $10). After receiving them, if I don't wish to receive any more books, I can return the shipping statement marked "cancel." If I don't cancel, I will receive 6 brand-new novels every month and be billed just $4.55 per book in the U.S. or $5.24 per book in Canada. That's a savings of at least 13% off the cover price! It's quite a bargain! Shipping and handling is just 50¢ per book in the U.S. and 75¢ per book in Canada.* I understand that accepting the 2 free books and gifts places me under no obligation to buy anything. I can always return a shipment and cancel at any time. Even if I never buy another book, the two free books and gifts are mine to keep forever.

225/326 HDN GH2P

Name _____ (PLEASE PRINT)

Address _____ Apt. #

City _____ State/Prov. _____ Zip/Postal Code

Signature (if under 18, a parent or guardian must sign)

Mail to the **Reader Service**:
IN U.S.A.: P.O. Box 1867, Buffalo, NY 14240-1867
IN CANADA: P.O. Box 609, Fort Erie, Ontario L2A 5X3

Want to try two free books from another line?
Call 1-800-873-8635 or visit www.ReaderService.com.

* Terms and prices subject to change without notice. Prices do not include applicable taxes. Sales tax applicable in N.Y. Canadian residents will be charged applicable taxes. Offer not valid in Quebec. This offer is limited to one order per household. Not valid for current subscribers to Harlequin Desire books. All orders subject to credit approval. Credit or debit balances in a customer's account(s) may be offset by any other outstanding balance owed by or to the customer. Please allow 4 to 6 weeks for delivery. Offer available while quantities last.

Your Privacy—The Reader Service is committed to protecting your privacy. Our Privacy Policy is available online at www.ReaderService.com or upon request from the Reader Service.

We make a portion of our mailing list available to reputable third parties that offer products we believe may interest you. If you prefer that we not exchange your name with third parties, or if you wish to clarify or modify your communication preferences, please visit us at www.ReaderService.com/consumerchoice or write to us at Reader Service Preference Service, P.O. Box 9062, Buffalo, NY 14240-9062. Include your complete name and address.

HDI5

SPECIAL EXCERPT FROM

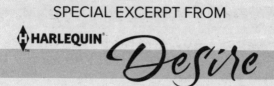
HARLEQUIN®
Desire

*Mac needs Andi. For work, that is. And when his
assistant quits on the spot to take a much-needed
break, he decides the only way to get her back is to do
whatever it takes to help her out.*

Read on for a sneak peek at
A BRIDE FOR THE BOSS
by USA TODAY bestselling author
Maureen Child, *part of the bestselling*
TEXAS CATTLEMAN'S CLUB *series!*

It had been a long day, but a good one.

Andi was feeling pretty smug about her decision to
quit her job and deliberately ignoring the occasional
twinges of regret. She should have done it three years
ago. As soon as she realized she was in love with a man
who would never see her as more than a piece of office
equipment.

Her heart ached a little, but she took another sip of
wine and purposefully drowned that pain. Once she was
free of her idle daydreams of Mac, she'd be able to look
around, find a man to be with. To help her build the life
she wanted so badly.

Her arms ached from wielding a paint roller, but
working on her home felt good. So good, in fact, she didn't
even grumble when someone knocked on the front door.

Wineglass in hand, she answered the door and jolted when Mac smiled at her.

"Mac? What're you doing here?"

"Hello to you, too," he said and stepped past her, unasked, into the house.

All she could do was close the door and follow him into the living room.

He turned around and gave her a quick smile that had her stomach jittering in response before she could quash her automatic response. "The color's good."

"Thanks. Mac, why are you here?"

"I'm here because I wanted to get a look at what you left me for." His gaze fixed on her and for the first time, he noticed that she wore a tiny tank top and a silky pair of drawstring pants. Her feet were bare and her toenails were painted a soft blush pink. Her hair was long and loose over her shoulders, just skimming the tops of her breasts.

Mac took a breath and wondered where that flash of heat had come from. He'd been with Andi nearly every day for the past six years and he'd never reacted to her like this before.

Now it seemed to be all he could notice.

Don't miss
A BRIDE FOR THE BOSS
by USA TODAY *bestselling author Maureen Child,*
available June 2016 wherever
Harlequin® Desire books and ebooks are sold.

www.Harlequin.com

Whatever You're Into... Passionate Reads

Looking for more passionate reads from Harlequin®?
Fear not! Harlequin® Presents, Harlequin® Desire and
Harlequin® Blaze offer you irresistible romance stories
featuring powerful heroes.

❦ HARLEQUIN *Presents*.

Do you want alpha males, decadent glamour and jet-set
lifestyles? Step into the sensational, sophisticated world of
Harlequin® Presents, where sinfully tempting heroes ignite a
fierce and wickedly irresistible passion!

❦ HARLEQUIN *Desire*

Harlequin® Desire novels are powerful, passionate and
provocative contemporary romances set against a backdrop of
wealth, privilege and sweeping family saga. Alpha heroes with
a soft side meet strong-willed but vulnerable heroines amid a
dramatic world of divided loyalties, high-stakes conflict and
intense emotion.

❦ HARLEQUIN *Blaze*.

Harlequin® Blaze stories sizzle with strong heroines and
irresistible heroes playing the game of modern love and lust.
They're fun, sexy and always steamy.

Be sure to check out our full selection of books
within each series every month!

www.Harlequin.com

HPASSION2016

HARLEQUIN®

A *Romance* FOR EVERY MOOD™

Love the Harlequin book you just read?

Your opinion matters.

Review this book on your favorite book site, review site, blog or your own social media properties and share your opinion with other readers!